GRAVE SHADOWS

GRAVE SHADOWS 5

TYNDALE KIDS

TYNDALE HOUSE PUBLISHERS, INC., CAROL STREAM, ILLINOIS

RED ROCK MYSTERIES

#1 BEST-SELLING AUTHORS

JERRY B. JENKINS · CHRIS FABRY

Visit Tyndale's exciting Web site for kids at www.tyndale.com/kids.

TYNDALE is a registered trademark of Tyndale House Publishers, Inc.

Tyndale Kids logo is a trademark of Tyndale House Publishers, Inc.

Grave Shadows

Designed by Jacqueline L. Nuñez

Edited by Lorie Popp

Published in association with the literary agency of Alive Communications, Inc., 7680 Goddard Street, Suite 200, Colorado Springs, CO 80920.

Scripture quotation are taken from the *Holy Bible*, New Living Translation, copyright © 1996, 2004. Used by permission of Tyndale House Publishers, Inc., Carol Stream, Illinois 60188. All rights reserved.

This novel is a work of fiction. Names, characters, places, and incidents either are the product of the authors' imagination or are used fictitiously. Any resemblance to actual events, locales, organizations, or persons, living or dead, is entirely coincidental and beyond the intent of either the authors or publisher.

For manufacturing information regarding this product, please call 1-800-323-9400.

Library of Congress Cataloging-in-Publication Data

Jenkins, Jerry B.
  Grave Shadows / Jerry B. Jenkins, Chris Fabry.
    p. cm. — (Red Rock mysteries ; 5)
  ISBN 978-1-4143-0144-0 (pbk.)
  [1. Bicycles and bicycling—Fiction. 2. Christian life—Fiction 3. Twins—Fiction. 4. Family life—
Colorado—Fiction. 5. Colorado—Fiction. 6. Mystery and detective stories.] I. Fabry, Chris, date. II. Title.
  PZ7+
  [Fic]—dc22   2005005292

Printed in the United States of America

16 15 14
 9   8   7   6   5

"O death, where is your **VICTORY?**
O death, where is your **STING?**"

1 CORINTHIANS 15:55

"**HOPE** is a **GOOD** thing,
maybe the BEST of things,
and no good thing ever dies."

FRANK DARABONT
The Shawshank Redemption

CHAPTER 1

☻ *Bryce* ☻

My friend Jeff Alexander was dying. We all knew it. I prayed God would perform a miracle, but I'm not sure I believed it would actually happen. When Jeff mentioned going to the graveyard near the haunted house, it made my skin crawl.

The hardest part of any cemetery is looking at the graves of kids. Did they get sick? fall down a well? The only thing you know is that they're sleeping with angels or in Jesus' arms—that's what the tombstones say.

That summer started out like most. Ashley and I were glad to be out of school and going into the eighth grade. She's my twin sister and likes to tell everybody she's older, but it's only by a few seconds. We can talk about everything but age.

Instead of just watching TV all day or bugging Mom for extra chores to make money, I told Jeff I'd ride with him on a bike hike. It was the least I could do since he has cancer. Sometimes he looks really good, like he'll live longer than us all. Then he has bad days.

Imagine a 200-mile bike ride. Made my butt numb just thinking about it. But it was for a good cause. Every mile meant more money for cancer research, and it was a chance to spend time with Jeff.

The plan was to start in Vail and ride through the mountains all the way to Colorado Springs. It wouldn't be easy, but my stepdad, Sam, says nothing really good in life is easy. I guess our family should really be good, because it's not easy living with two new people who don't believe the way you do. Sam and his daughter, Leigh, aren't Christians, and my mom and sister and I are. We have a little brother too, Dylan.

Sam's wife and younger daughter died in the same plane crash our dad died in. Sam met my mom at a memorial ceremony, and they fell in love. That was before Mom became a Christian. We moved from Illinois to Colorado, which is probably the biggest change in scenery imaginable. Instead of everything being as flat as a paper plate, there were mountains all around, thin air, animals, snow in April and May, and no Cubs games. It was a shock, but Ashley and I got used to it.

The bike trip was a week away when Jeff suggested the graveyard trip. Ashley and her friend Hayley said they wanted to go too, and I figured the more the merrier.

That's when things got interesting.

CHAPTER 2

✖ Ashley ✖

"Do you believe in ghosts?" Hayley said as we pedaled up a hill behind Bryce and Jeff. They were riding a tandem, a two-person bike. Hayley and I were on separate bikes. It was getting really hot and hard to keep going.

"You mean dead people coming back?" I said, trying to catch my breath.

"Yeah, people who haunt you." She let out a "Wooooooooo!" then said, "I saw this TV show where they recorded an actual ghost walking through a room. There were a couple of kids asleep in bunk beds, and through the dark you saw this misty green thing move past them, stop, then walk right through the wall."

Bryce and Jeff were so far ahead they couldn't hear us. They were going really slow, like they might have to stop any minute.

"It was probably just special effects," I said.

"No, they put a camera up and didn't touch it the whole night. I couldn't sleep for a week after I saw that."

The story gave me goose bumps, or maybe that was just my body shutting down. We were in the third mile of a five-mile ride to the end of Red Lake Canyon, a dirt road that winds around the side of the mountain until it flattens at the top. Bryce and I had never actually been to the very end, and we were both excited to see the haunted house.

"There are no such things as ghosts," I said. "When you die, that's it. You don't come back and hang around little kids in their bedrooms."

"Then what did I see on that show?"

I hit my brakes and stopped by the side of the road. Empty Mountain Dew bottles littered the washed-out rut, along with a Sonic Styrofoam cup and an old tire. Colorado's a pretty state and people usually take care of things, but I guess when they get this far they forget where they live.

Hayley had been to our church a few times, but I was sure she wasn't a Christian. And I didn't want to just spout stuff my mom told me. "All I know is that the Bible never says people who die come back and haunt us."

Usually when I mention the Bible or Jesus, Hayley gets quiet or changes the subject. Lately she's seemed more interested.

"What does it say then?" she said.

"That we only get one chance. We don't come back as a frog or a tree, another person, or a ghost. After we die, God judges us, and the most important thing is what we do with Jesus."

Jeff let out an exhausted yell from in front of us. "I have to stop."

CHAPTER 3

☾ *Bryce* ☾

I stopped, and Jeff and I stood panting. We were almost to the flat part of the road, but I've learned that when Jeff yells you have to stop.

When I first heard about Jeff's cancer, it made me want to run from him. It was painful to see him get weaker, lose his hair, walk funny. Mrs. Ogilvie, our counselor at church, helped me see Jeff needed friends the same as everybody else. The only reason I wanted to run was because I didn't want to lose another person in my life, like my dad.

Being friends with somebody who's sick is like trying to pull a stubborn tooth. It's hard at first, but the more you pull and the more painful it gets, the better it feels when the thing's actually out of your mouth. Except there's no cancer fairy, though I wish there were.

"Can we walk the bike the rest of the way to the top?" Jeff said, still panting. He had on a backpack that looked like it weighed more than he did.

"Sure," I said.

Ashley and Hayley caught up and walked their bikes too. I guess so we wouldn't feel bad. Jeff and I had been riding the Santa Fe Trail, an old railroad line that's been turned into a bike and running track. It goes for miles and miles, but we've worked up to 10 miles each way. That's on flat ground. Riding in the mountains is different.

"What about you, Bryce?" Hayley said. "You don't think there're any ghosts back at this old cemetery, do you?"

I shook my head. "Don't believe in 'em."

"I've been coming here for months," Jeff said when he caught his breath. I wondered how we were going to ride 200 miles up and down hills when he couldn't even go five without gasping. "I haven't seen anything at the cemetery except for deer and a few foxes."

The farther we climbed, the rougher the road got. There were washed-out sections and deep ruts.

"How do you get back here?" Ashley said.

"Dad drives. We built a tree house near the cemetery. Can't wait for you to see it."

When we got to the top of the hill, we stopped in the shade and took out our water bottles. A car rumbled past, kicking up a lot of dust, and I smelled something that made me think I'd never eat another bite in my life.

Hayley groaned. "What's that stink?"

Ashley pulled her shirt over her nose and pointed to the edge of the road.

"Skunk pancake," Jeff said.

He was right. A car had flattened a skunk, and it looked and smelled like it had been there for days. We moved past it, and the girls turned their heads.

"Roadkill-a-rama!" Jeff said.

I added, "Flattened where he ran!" and I thought Hayley was going to kill us.

Something about the skunk wasn't really so funny, though. It gave me a bad feeling.

CHAPTER 4

❀ Ashley ❀

The rest of the ride wasn't as hard because the road flattened.
Every now and then we'd get a view down the mountain through a
break in the trees, and it looked like something you'd see on a bro-
chure about visiting Colorado.

Pinecones dotted the road, and black squirrels with pointy ears
darted back and forth. There weren't many houses back here, but
the ones we found were either plain and simple or mansions. A little
gravel driveway might lead to a trailer with old cars out front. The
next driveway might wind down a hill to a house that looked like a
palace with a tennis court or a pool.

We also saw beer cans and cigarette lighters thrown about. I'd heard that teenagers came out here to party at night. Old newspapers blew around with other trash. When Hayley spotted a DQ cup she said, "I could go for a grape Mr. Misty right now."

Some of the trees didn't look healthy. Only pine trees and aspens grow at this altitude, but the tops of the pines were brown, like they were dying. Maybe it was just the time of year or the invading pine beetles, but the decaying trees made me think of Jeff.

Barbed wire ran along the edge of the road, going from tree to tree. Several horses stood by the fence and seemed to watch us, their backs twitching and tails swishing at flies.

"There it is!" Hayley said.

CHAPTER 5

☺ *Bryce* ☺

The house loomed above us like it was attached to the clouds. The deep blue sky made its faded shutters and peeling paint look more dingy. It looked like something out of a scary movie where people get stranded and are chased by some maniac.

The trees opened and bordered the house like a picture frame. Weeds and thistles covered the front yard—if you could call it that. An aspen grove had taken over one side of the hill.

"The graves are over there," Jeff said, gesturing through the trees to a spot past the house.

I cringed as we rode past. I'd heard so many stories about people who had been killed, gold prospectors who haunted the grounds, and more. A well in front of the house had a graying bucket at its edge.

"Keep going," Jeff said.

We pedaled to a rickety picket fence at the end of the road and parked our bikes. We walked into the graveyard, shaded by some of the largest pine trees I had ever seen. I checked my watch. We had gone five miles, but it had taken more than two hours, and if we were to be back home in time for dinner like we'd promised, we'd have to leave soon.

Jeff carried his backpack and led us to the end of the graveyard, pointing out the oldest markers. One had a simple wooden cross and looked a thousand years old. It was actually from 1904, and Jeff said it marked the grave of the son of a man we had studied about in Colorado history.

He trotted to the fence, climbed over it, and stood in front of a tree that rose like a monster. Planks had been nailed directly into the trunk. Ashley and Hayley looked skittish, but Jeff led the way and we scampered up.

CHAPTER 6

❈ Ashley ❈

The view from the road was something, but the scene from the tree house was amazing. It was like we were on top of the world. Jeff and his dad had nailed a railing around the tree house so no one would fall. We could see the town of Red Rock in the distance, houses dotting the landscape like pieces on a Monopoly board.

To our right Pikes Peak spread like a brown masterpiece. Straight ahead stood the spires of the Air Force Academy Chapel. Past that was Colorado Springs.

"Ever been here at night?" Bryce said.

Jeff's eyes sparkled. "You should see it. A million lights flicker. Kind of makes it okay that we don't have fireflies around here."

Jeff seemed energized, as if just being here gave him life. He pointed out other places he recognized and even showed us where our house was by identifying the red rocks behind our property.

We drank from our water bottles, and Bryce climbed down and got our lunches from the bikes.

Jeff just picked at his food, taking some pills with his sandwich. He pulled out a pad of paper and jotted a few things. "It's for my column," he said.

"Great, we're going to be famous," Hayley said, chuckling.

One of Jeff's dreams was to be a writer, and with the help of the local newspaper he had become one. "Jeff's Diary" carried his weekly thoughts and experiences. Sometimes it was funny, other times sad. Everybody I knew read it, even if they didn't read anything else in the paper.

Bryce seemed focused on the haunted house.

"See any ghosts?" Hayley said.

Bryce turned, his face pale. "I thought I saw someone in that upstairs window."

CHAPTER 7

☉ *Bryce* ☉

Sometimes it's weird what you think you see when you're scared. I didn't want to notice anything in that upstairs window. Could it have been the wind moving the shutters? Was someone there? What were they doing in that spooky old house?

"You guys investigate," Jeff said. "I'll stay here."

Ashley and Hayley and I climbed down and walked up the old driveway, which looked like it had been made for a horse and buggy. We skirted the front and stopped at an old outbuilding that looked like it was home to a bunch of snakes.

Shutters hung at weird angles from the house. A balcony with a crumbling railing ran around the top floor. All the windows were broken. You'd have to throw a rock for at least a year to hit any glass.

"You guys scared of dying?" Hayley whispered.

We looked at her like she was playing with the dead skunk.

"No, I mean like Jeff. He doesn't seem scared at all."

"Can we talk about this later?" I said. "Besides, he's not going to die."

Hayley nodded and moved to the front of the little building. The half-moon cut into the door told me this had been an outhouse—an outdoor bathroom. I'd read about them but had never actually seen one. I peeked inside at a long bench with a hole cut in it.

"Let's go in the house," Hayley said.

"Thought you were afraid to die," I said. I didn't want to hurt Hayley's feelings, but she was getting on my nerves.

"We should see who's in there," she said.

I stepped onto the back porch. Weeds grew through the floor. The boards creaked and we stopped, listening.

"What if drug dealers are inside?" Ashley whispered. "Somebody said there used to be a bunch of hippies living here."

"What's a hippie?" Hayley said.

"Quiet," I said.

The screen door at the back squeaked and nearly fell off. The back door wasn't locked, so I went inside. My heart beat like a drum during the 1812 Overture, but I didn't want the girls to know it.

I had no idea why I was doing this, but I was going to do it anyway. The old kitchen was buried under dust on the table and every chair. Through holes in the floor you could see into the cellar, which I didn't really want to do.

"Maybe this isn't such a good idea," Ashley said.

I moved to the living room. There was an old piano with the

bench toppled over. Spiderwebs reached from one end of the entry to the other. I pointed to a black widow and told the girls, "You don't want to get bitten by one of those."

Dust danced in the shafts of sunlight streaming through the front window. Huge cracks in the ceiling ran the length of the living room, and it looked like the light fixture was ready to fall.

"Somebody's up there," Hayley whispered.

CHAPTER 8

❀ Ashley ❀

I felt like running. Hayley put her arm around me, and we followed Bryce, as if drawn by some unseen force.

Jeff had said this house had belonged to an old prospector named John Bascom and that gold was hidden somewhere on the grounds. Whoever found it would be rich beyond their wildest dreams. From all the holes in the walls and floor it looked like somebody had searched every inch of the place.

Bryce stepped onto the creaky stairs and stopped when something thumped above us. Was someone trying to get away?

"Hello?" Bryce said.

No answer.

He motioned to a missing stair and stepped over it. Hayley and I were side by side now, not willing to let go of each other. Bryce reached the top first, two stairs at a time.

Suddenly a step gave way, the wood cracking beneath Hayley and me. I grabbed the railing and her arm as her leg punched through. She screamed.

Bryce edged back down and helped me pull Hayley up. Her leg was scratched, but there was no blood.

We finally reached a long hallway, and Bryce pointed at a door. Before we reached it, the door flew open.

"Hi, guys!" Jeff said, laughing.

"How did you—?"

"Secret entrance," he said. "My dad and I have been through this house lots of times."

Jeff showed us a narrow staircase that went straight down to a door to the outside.

Hayley stopped. "Look."

In the corner sat a paper bag with a King Soopers' grocery store logo on it. She picked it up.

"What's special about an empty bag?" Jeff said.

Hayley shrugged.

"There's no dust on it," I said. "Somebody's just been here."

CHAPTER 9

⋃ *Bryce* ⋃

As we got on our bikes, Jeff turned back to the cemetery. "I asked my dad if they'd let me be buried up here."

I rolled my eyes. "Stop talking that way."

"I'd love to be planted up here." He pointed to Pikes Peak. "Picture yourself with your wife and kids, coming back here. You could show them this house, talk about this summer. Maybe your mom would even write a story about us."

"I want to be buried near the interstate where people can build a big monument for me," I said. "They can honk and throw flowers out their windows as they pass."

Jeff stuck his tongue out and blew air through his teeth. It was his unique way of laughing that I never got tired of. Once in history class while he was giving a report he said something funny and started to laugh, then couldn't stop. He just kept blowing air and sticking his tongue out, and the whole class had a hard time not laughing the rest of the hour.

Going down the hill was a lot easier than coming up, but the way Jeff panted, then didn't even pedal, made me wonder about our trip.

When we got past the skunk who had passed to his eternal reward, Jeff stopped to rest.

"I have an idea," I said.

"Shoot."

"There are a bunch of riders, right?"

"More than a hundred."

"And we're riding over some main roads, right?"

"Some back roads, but mostly the main ones."

"What if we took our ATVs and rode behind them—you know, to bring up the rear and help out people who need it."

Jeff's jaw dropped so low I thought he was going to dig gravel on the side of the road. "I'm not riding an ATV behind everybody. No way."

I held up both hands. "It was just an idea."

He stared at me with such intensity that I had to look away. "Look, Bryce, this is what I've dreamed about ever since the doctor said I was sick. I've had the chance to go to Disneyland or Disney World or a hundred other places sick kids go. I don't want to do that. I don't want to shake the president's hand or eat dinner with some famous athlete who pities me."

"I get the point—"

"I don't want to go to the Grand Canyon or surf in Hawaii, not that I could surf anyway. . . ." He took his Rockies cap off, and the sun glinted off his bald head. "This is what I want to do. I've dreamed of it for months. I can see the finish line. But if there's any part of you that doesn't want to—"

"I do want to go," I said. "I'm just worried you'll get sicker or that we won't make it. I'm with you until the end, even if you have to drag me the last few miles."

Jeff smiled. "Yeah, I just might have to drag your sorry carcass across that finish line."

"You're going to be riding in front when we do cross," I said.

He laughed with his tongue stuck out.

It was the best sound I'd heard all day.

CHAPTER 10

✿ Ashley ✿

Hayley and I cycled ahead while Bryce and Jeff stopped. The sun cast deep shadows on the road, and it felt good to have the wind in our faces as we coasted. The wheels *click-click-click*ed as we wound our pedals backward, bouncing along the uneven road.

I wanted to talk to Hayley more about God, and though no time seemed right, I could tell something was bothering her.

"What do you think will happen to Jeff?" she said, looking over her shoulder.

"One day at a time. That's what Bryce says. The doctors don't really know."

"I feel sorry for him. Can't imagine what it's like for his parents. Kind of reminds me what my aunt's going through."

"Your aunt?"

"My cousin disappeared a couple of weeks ago. He called in to work, told them he'd be there in a half hour, then never made it."

I had read something about it in the paper but hadn't paid much attention. Now that I knew it was Hayley's cousin, I was a lot more interested.

"He has a little dog that goes everywhere with him," Hayley continued. "He left the dog locked up. My aunt found the poor thing and let her out. The dog's been whimpering and crying ever since."

"Strange." A million questions shot through my mind. I asked where he was last seen, if he was in any kind of trouble, and if he'd ever disappeared before. Finally I said, "What kind of car does he drive?"

"Yellow Jeep. He loves it as much as the dog. Always washing and polishing it."

"Police say anything?"

"They don't have a clue."

CHAPTER 11

☺ *Bryce* ☺

We rode our brakes the rest of the way and avoided loose rocks. After talking with Jeff, I was going to finish the ride no matter what.

We waved good-bye to Ashley and Hayley and headed for Jeff's house. The training we had gone through the past two weeks had made my legs stronger, and it felt like I was really getting into shape. Don't get me wrong. I wasn't about to go on the Tour de France, but I knew I would do better at higher altitudes.

We parked the tandem bike in Jeff's garage, washed the dirt off, and made sure it was oiled.

Mrs. Alexander called Jeff inside for his medicine. "Bryce, I wanted to tell you of a development," she said when he was gone.

"Development?"

She sat on a lawn chair and lowered her voice. "We have a room set aside for some of the things Jeff's been given. Signed baseballs, autographs . . ."

I had seen the room. People had sent him pictures, tickets, and memorabilia I was sure were worth lots of money. Even one of Barry Bonds' record-breaking home-run baseballs.

"Some of the most expensive items are missing," she said.

"Missing?"

She nodded. "We told Jeff we're having the carpet cleaned and locked the door so he wouldn't see."

"Who would take that stuff?"

She shook her head. "We were hoping you might help. We don't want Jeff to know—he'll be gone for the bike trip in a couple of days."

"So will I. Maybe Ashley can help. When did you notice the things missing?"

Mrs. Alexander guessed the thefts had happened within the past two days. "We've had people bringing food, a woman to do some housework, people like that."

"Any of Jeff's friends?"

She was about to answer when Jeff came back into the garage. She smiled at him.

"Mom, you should have seen us today. We're going to make this trip in record time."

I felt good that Jeff was so positive, but all I could think was, who would have stolen a sick kid's memorabilia?

CHAPTER 12

❀ Ashley ❀

Bryce set a list in front of me that Mrs. Alexander had given him of the things she knew were missing.

John Elway signed football
Framed letters from several movie stars, including Tom Hanks and Tom Cruise
Barry Bonds home-run ball
Signed riding bib from Lance Armstrong
Hockey puck from the Colorado Avalanche
Signed basketball from Denver Nugget Carmelo Anthony

I blew air through my lips. "Somebody had to back a truck up for all this stuff."

"It's an armload," Bryce said. "I think they passed the stuff out through the window."

"They?"

"Could be one person, I guess," he said. "But it's a lot of stuff."

"Could somebody climb inside through the window?"

Bryce shook his head. "They keep it locked. But if somebody opened it from the inside, they could let someone else in."

Bryce and I talked of how he could get information from Jeff while on their bike trip without tipping him off that his things had been stolen.

"I'm going to help Hayley with her missing cousin while you're gone," I said.

"Two cases at once," Bryce said. "Think you can handle it?"

"I'm sure going to try."

CHAPTER 13

☺ *Bryce* ☺

After church, Sam drove me to Jeff's house. We were supposed to go supply shopping for the trip, but he told Jeff he had a surprise.

"What is it?" Jeff said.

"You'll see," Sam said, winking at Mrs. Alexander.

She slipped me a sheet of paper when we arrived. When we left I let Jeff sit in the front so I could open the paper in the backseat, out of his sight.

Several names were on the sheet, people who had been in the house over the past week. I recognized Denise, a flute player in the band. There was a volunteer nurse and a few people from their church. I penciled in Boo Heckler just because he was such a nasty kid. He'd been sent to juvenile detention not long ago, but I'd heard he was already out.

Jeff turned around. "Whatcha reading?"

"Nothing to speak of," I said, stuffing the paper in my pocket.

Sam still wouldn't tell us where we were going, but when we headed north on I-25 I guessed he was taking us to his airplane hangar. Sam's a charter pilot, flying people wherever they need to go. Sometimes they're celebrities or athletes, or it could be businesspeople or whoever can afford it. I keep hoping he'll be asked to fly a famous preacher or evangelist so they'll say something that will make him become a Christian.

Sam was showing us his plane when he said, "Buckle up," and he climbed into the cockpit.

Jeff's eyes grew wide. "Are you actually taking us up?"

Sam smiled. "Want to show you something."

CHAPTER 14

✽ Ashley ✽

Hayley's aunt looked like one of those old Victorian writers my mom has a picture of on the wall of her office. Brown hair framing a narrow face. Long nose. Thin lips. Brown eyes that seem to pierce you.

She invited us inside but didn't offer us anything to eat or drink like my mom would do. The house was cluttered with magazines and newspapers. *Disheveled.* That's a word from a book we read in English. The house wasn't a rat's nest, but it was close.

"Ashley wants to help us find Gunnar," Hayley said.

The woman's face fell.

I heard scratching from the other room. Hayley opened the door and let a little dog out. She came right to me and bared her teeth—not that she was going to bite, more like she was smiling.

"That's right, Jenny," Hayley's aunt said. "Say hello to Ashley." Jenny nuzzled my hand and sat by my side.

The woman repeated the story. Gunnar had phoned work in Colorado Springs to say he was running late, then never showed up. "He sells pool tables and those hot tub things," she said. "He was always reliable, always on time as far as I know. I'm worried sick about him."

"Did he act strange before he disappeared?" I said. "Nervous or upset?"

"Not that I remember. He said he might look for a new job that paid more, but he wouldn't just run off because of that."

"What about his friends?" I said.

"He still has friends from high school," she said, looking at Hayley. "You remember the Baldwin boy, Darren. They'd go to ball games together. But he seemed . . ." She got a far-off look in her eyes.

"What? This might help."

"He just seemed preoccupied—spacey. Like there was something going on he didn't want me to know about. He always took good care of Jenny, so when he left her locked up, I got suspicious. That was almost two weeks ago." She held a tissue to her face.

"Where is his room?" I said.

"He has an apartment over the garage," Hayley said.

"Mind if we take a look, ma'am?" I said.

The woman waved, and we walked outside through gravel to the detached garage. I wondered what a 20-something guy was doing still living at home with his mom. I want to move out as soon as I'm 18.

His apartment was like a poster for tornado damage. Double disheveled. Clothes piled on a ratty couch, dog hair everywhere, dishes in the sink. Trash can overflowing.

"What if he comes back and finds us?" Hayley said.

"How could he find us in all this?" I said, looking through mail stacked on a small desk. I searched for any kind of clue—a doctor's report that he had some incurable disease, medicine that would knock him out, signs of a struggle—but I came up empty. Talking with Gunnar's high school pal might be a start.

CHAPTER 15

☺ *Bryce* ☺

Sam took off and my stomach fell. It's that first rush of lifting off the ground that's strange. Jeff was staring out the window. "5,281, 82, 83 . . . ," he said, pretending to announce our altitude after taking off from the Mile High City.

"You're not going to do that the whole trip, are you?" I said, smiling.

We headed west toward the mountains with Sam pointing out the stadiums where the Rockies and Broncos play. As we rose, Denver took on the look of a lot of cities. A haze shrouded the buildings.

Cars looked like they were going in slow motion, and the roads looked like a Mattel racetrack.

"Where are we going, Mr. Timberline?" Jeff said.

"Your route," Sam said.

Jeff conked himself on the forehead with the heel of a hand. "What a great idea."

We followed Interstate 70 into the mountains and were soon over the starting place for our bike trip. Jeff was going to spend a night at a camp where people with cancer relax and have fun. I would join him the next day.

The camp sat in the middle of a big forest surrounded by ski runs.

Sam said in his growly voice, "The bike trail runs along that stream—"

"I see it!" Jeff shouted. "Looks just like I thought."

Sam banked left and followed the roads and paths we would take through the first leg of our journey. It didn't look difficult from the air, but sometimes looks can fool you.

Sam flew low along the mountains, and every glance at the rocks and trees looked like a different page from a nature calendar. Huge slabs of rock rose out of the earth like castles, and I wondered what ·it would look like from the ground.

Sam pointed out a town where we would stop. Then we headed south toward Buena Vista. We flew over a campground—another planned stop—and soared through a valley that stretched for miles.

"I admire you guys for even attempting this," Sam said.

"You should see all the sponsors I'm getting," Jeff said. "With all the pledges so far, I'll make $25,000 for the research fund if we finish."

"Put me down for a dollar a mile," Sam said.

Jeff smiled and scribbled on a pad of paper.

Sam dipped lower, and the ground came rushing up at us.

"Buffalo!" Jeff yelled.

A herd grazed in an open field. They must have been used to low-flying planes because we didn't seem to bother them.

A yellow car pulled into a gas station on a lonely stretch of road, and I thought about Hayley's cousin. Was he out here somewhere, lost and alone? Had he been banged on the head and forgotten his name?

Sam flew over Wilkerson Pass, one of my favorite places in the whole state. He showed us where we'd ride, winding through Woodland Park. We flew over the Garden of the Gods, where we'd finish. My legs were tired just looking at the route.

Jeff beamed. "Think of crossing the finish line. It's going to be the best thing I'll ever do in my life."

Fear washed over me. What if I was the one who couldn't finish? What if I let Jeff down?

CHAPTER 16

JEFF'S DIARY

by Jeff Alexander

I'd like to welcome Colorado Springs readers to my column. My name is Jeff Alexander, and I'm like any 13-year-old kid, except I have cancer. This weekend is the biggest of my life because I'm riding 200 miles in a bike hike with my friend Bryce. A store donated a special bike we can ride together, and we're really looking forward to it.

By the time you read this, I'll be on the road, pedaling my feet off and breathing the fresh Colorado air. You can't begin to understand how excited I am. I've been waiting and hoping for this for months, and now it's finally here.

The great thing is, lots of people are sponsoring me for 25 cents a mile or even a few dollars a mile, and all the money goes to cancer research. In the hospital kids just like me are fighting for their lives, but you'd never know it. They're really neat people who just have something wrong with them.

I've learned a lot over the past few months about what's important, what's not important, and to make every day count. I believe God gives us life for a reason, and when we get sick, he can use that too. (If you don't believe in God, that's okay. I just hope you give him a chance, because he really loves you a lot.)

People ask me sometimes what it's like to not know how much longer you're going to live. My dad let me see part of the movie *Braveheart* once where William Wallace says, "Every man dies; not every man really lives." Whether I die in 50 years or 50 days, I want people to say that I really lived.

So if you see a lot of bikes and people wearing the same blue and red shirts, slow down and wave. We're just people who want to really live and help others do the same.

CHAPTER 17

✖ Ashley ✖

I found out that Darren Baldwin works at the RadioShack in Red Rock, in a little strip mall near some restaurants. Before dinner I rode my ATV close to town and walked the rest of the way.

The sun, which is almost always out where we live, was staying up longer. Kids rode bikes on the middle school parking lot, trying to jump over a wood ramp they'd set up. Others played baseball behind the school.

The RadioShack sat between Red Rock Donuts and Spotless Dry Cleaners. A sign read Summer Blowout Sale. The store was packed with electronic gadgets, remote-control cars, TVs, batteries, computers, and every cable and plug ever invented.

An older man behind the counter looked over his glasses and asked if he could help me.

I felt like I should buy something, especially if I was going to ask questions. I touched the battery display. "I need double As for my CD player."

He came out from behind the counter and recommended a package. I looked at the price and gulped, then grabbed the smallest one. "Darren working today?" I said.

The man's eyebrows went up. "As a matter of fact he is. Darren?"

Darren ducked as he came through the low-hung door. He was thin and had a fair complexion, with freckles and white skin, and sandy red hair. His long arms reminded me of a jazz piano player I had seen on TV.

I introduced myself and said, "I hear you're a friend of Gunnar Roberts."

"Known him since we were kids. Why?"

"I'm trying to help find him. Any idea where he could be?"

Darren looked at the manager, and the man must have nodded or something because Darren relaxed. He pointed to a stool in the other room, and I sat. A computer lay on a workbench with lots of tools spread around. "Haven't talked with Gunnar for a few weeks," Darren said. "It's like he disappeared off the face of the earth."

"When was the last time you saw him?"

"Went to a Rockies game. Sat in the Rockpile and tried to get a tan. I just got burned."

"He didn't say anything about leaving?"

He shook his head. "We talked about our jobs, girlfriend stuff."

"He has a girlfriend?"

"Taryn broke up with him. He said she was really ticked."

"Ticked enough to hurt him?"

He shrugged. "Never thought of that."

I wrote down her name, and Darren told me where she lived. He chuckled. "You a junior detective or something?"

If I had a nickel for every time I heard that . . . "You think Gunnar could have done something to himself? Was he that upset about this girl?"

He frowned. "Kill himself? Nah. He was squirrelly, always has been. But he wouldn't do anything like that."

"What do you mean, squirrelly?"

"He'd go off for a couple of days, and we wouldn't know where he was. Take his dog and hike or go up in the mountains four-wheeling, I guess. He never told me what he did."

"He have problems at work?"

"Didn't like his job, but he needed the money for car payments. He always talked about winning the lottery."

The store manager moved around behind us, and Darren shifted in his chair.

"I'd better go," I said, standing and moving to the front counter. Darren followed and took the money for the batteries. "Any idea where he might have gone in the mountains?"

He shook his head.

"Was his Jeep muddy when he came back?"

He thought for a minute as he handed me my change. "He kept that thing spotless. I don't ever remember him coming back with dirt on it."

I thanked him and left. I looked back as I walked through the parking lot and saw Darren watching me through the window.

CHAPTER 18

◑ *Bryce* ◑

The next day was Jeff's dad's turn for a surprise. Just as Jeff and I were hitting the driveway on the bike, he pulled in front of us, hopped out, and grabbed something from the backseat. "These just came in. Try them on."

"Dad, we already have helmets," Jeff said.

"Not like these," he said.

They looked like regular helmets, except they had little microphones. "You guys won't have to yell at each other during your rides with these."

We pulled the helmets on and flicked the switch for the microphone. I could hear every word Jeff said, even when he whispered.

We thanked his dad, and as we pedaled away I said, "Pretty neat, huh?"

"Dad's having a hard time."

"What do you mean?"

"He didn't want me to do this bike trip until Mom convinced him. I guess he's entitled to have a hard time, though. Dad's gotta let go of me a lot sooner than most."

Jeff talked about his dad until we reached the Santa Fe Trail.

"Ready to kick up some dust?" I said.

"Hit it," Jeff said.

We flew down the trail all the way to the Air Force Academy. The ride back was harder, especially for Jeff, but we made it in our fastest time yet. The trip was a little farther than we'd ride our first full day.

We stopped to have a drink. Each day I was feeling stronger, and my rear was getting used to the seat. Jeff went into a jiffy toilet and kept his helmet on. We found we could walk a long way away from each other and still talk through the microphones. I asked if there'd been any weird people at his house helping the family.

"That Denise girl is strange," he said. "I don't know why she comes over. She doesn't want to be there—either her parents make her or she thinks bringing food to sick people will help her get into heaven."

"How often does she come?"

"Every few days. And then there's the lady who cleans our place. Mom says her family's pretty poor. She takes one look at me and starts crying. I just go to my room when she shows up."

CHAPTER 19

✖ Ashley ✖

I met Hayley at Red Rock Lake, about halfway between our houses. We sat in the gazebo and fed the ducks bread crumbs. The lake's been fed by an underground spring, and they've never had problems. But this year something must have happened to the spring because the water level keeps going down. They finally decided to just drain the whole thing.

I told Hayley what I had found out from Darren. She pulled out her cell phone and called information for the number of Gunnar's old girlfriend, Taryn. She wrote it down and handed it to me.

"Before we call, I need to know if you're serious about finding your cousin."

"Of course. Why wouldn't I be?"

"Because it took you a while to even tell me about it. And some things bother me about this. He left without his dog. Didn't tell his mother anything. Told the people where he worked he would be right there and then didn't show up. There's a chance that something really bad happened."

"Knowing is a lot better than not knowing."

I dialed Taryn's number, and an answering machine picked up. I asked her to call me and left my home number.

Hayley walked to the water's edge and rooted around in the mud with a stick. She held up a chain with something on the end of it. "An old watch!" she shouted.

I took a closer look. "Somebody must have dropped it out of their boat years ago."

"This thing could be worth lots of money."

"Maybe."

The sun glinted off the lake's surface, and something moved in the water, a huge fin passing in front of us. We stepped back.

Hayley said, "Let's come back tomorrow and look for coins and stuff. My dad has a metal detector."

"I have to watch Dylan tomorrow," I said.

"Bring him along."

As I walked back to my ATV I turned to take one more look at the lake. Something yellow, submerged in the deep end, cut through the murky darkness and caught the sunlight. A cloud passed and it was gone.

Was it just the sun playing tricks?

CHAPTER 20

☺ *Bryce* ☺

I beat Ashley to the ringing phone after dinner, but it was for her. I went to my room to study a map of the roads and trails Jeff and I would take on the bike trip.

I'm not what you'd call a spiritual giant or anything, but I try to read something from the Bible every day and pray. To be honest, during the school year it's hard to get up early, and in the summer I want to sleep in. I feel guilty about it, like if I don't spend time with God he'll hate me and give me some disease like Jeff has. I know that's not true, but still . . .

I opened my Bible to Proverbs. Mom told me once that if I read one proverb every day I'd be as wise as Solomon. I said, "Who's Solomon?" Now I know, of course.

There are 31 proverbs, so sometimes I read the proverb that's the same as the day of the month, but this time I just found the nearest one. It was the 17th proverb and I stopped at the 17th verse: "A friend is always loyal, and a brother is born to help in time of need."

I felt like a brother to Jeff. Everything I had gone through with my dad dying had prepared me to be a better friend than I would have been otherwise.

I copied the verse onto a small sheet of paper and read it over and over. The best thing I could do for Jeff was try and find his missing stuff. I wrote a list of suspects and tried to think of my next move. I was about to pray when Ashley came in.

"Who was on the phone?" I said.

She frowned and plopped onto my beanbag chair. "Gunnar's ex-girlfriend. I thought she could help figure out where he might be."

"She didn't give you anything?"

"Said they broke up a month ago. She was tired of being strung along, and he wasn't ready to move out of his mom's place."

"Sounds like she was more serious about him than he was about her."

Ashley stared at the ceiling. "Yeah, but she did say she talked with him a couple weeks ago and he acted weird."

"Weird?"

"She called about something she had left at his house, and Gunnar sounded scared and said he'd call her back. He never did."

"What could he be scared of?"

Ashley shrugged. "I've got a bad feeling. I wonder if anybody will ever see him alive again."

CHAPTER 21

❦ Ashley ❦

Mom dropped Dylan and me at Hayley's house, and we walked to Red Rock Lake. I told Hayley what Taryn had said, and I could tell it upset her. I had made a mental list of all the things I thought could have happened to Gunnar, from being robbed or kidnapped to hurting himself. I hoped he would turn up at his mom's house and apologize for scaring her, but I wasn't holding my breath.

Dylan tagged along as we walked down to the lakeshore. He was interested in the metal detector.

Hayley winked at me and tossed a coin on the ground behind Dylan. "Want to try it?" she said.

His eyes lit up, and he grabbed the thing so fast I thought he would tear it apart. She helped him hold it, and when the thing beeped, he almost came out of his skin. He held up the quarter like it was a billion dollars, and I couldn't help laughing.

Hayley explored a sandy place at the end of the lake, swinging the metal detector from side to side. She found fishing lures on old logs exposed by the receding water. When she got a strong beep, Dylan and I helped her dig up a gun.

"Wonder why this is in here," Hayley said.

"Looks really old. I'm not sure we'll ever know."

She found a 1963 class ring from Red Rock High School, two knives, a tackle box, and several coins as we walked back and forth along the bank.

Suddenly I looked around and couldn't see Dylan. I figured he had moved up to the playground, but when I got there, I didn't see him.

I heard a scream and looked across the lake. Dylan was waist-deep in mud and sinking.

CHAPTER 22

◑ *Bryce* ◑

While Jeff's mom took him to a doctor's appointment to get final approval for going on the bike trip, his dad unlocked the trophy-room door for me. He was leaving for work and asked if I would mind letting in the housekeeper when she arrived.

He paused. "I can't tell you how much we appreciate your helping Jeff with the bike trip. To tell you the truth, I wish he'd stay home and rest." I could tell he was fighting tears.

"I'll take good care of him," I said.

"I know." He put a hand on my shoulder. "It's just so hard not knowing what's going to happen with him after that." It seemed he had more to say, but his voice caught.

"Mr. Alexander," I said, "Jeff knows how much you love him."

He nodded and hurried out to his car.

The trophy room looked almost bare with so much stuff gone. A glass case, like you see in jewelry stores, had empty baseball and basketball holders inside. What was left were things like a signed CD from a female singer Jeff hated and things like that.

The window was locked, and there was no other way into the room. The closet had a few games on the shelf and some old suitcases, but nothing else. An opening led to the attic, but I wondered who would know about that or want to go to all that trouble. I locked the door and left the room.

The doorbell rang and I let in the housekeeper, a thin woman with dark hair. She carried supplies in a plastic bucket.

"I thought only rich people had housekeepers," I said, smiling. She said she had found out about the Alexanders at church and was donating her services every two weeks.

"Have you ever cleaned the trophy room?"

She shook her head. "They told me not to bother with it. Never been in there."

CHAPTER 23

❦ Ashley ❦

I ran toward Dylan with Hayley right on my heels. What would I tell Mom about his clothes? When I got to him and saw how deep he had sunk in the mud, I forgot about the clothes.

"Hang on, Dylan!" I screamed, slipping on the bank. I went down hard, then scrambled up again.

Dylan was pale, his eyes huge, big tears running down his cheeks. He flailed, and the mud inched toward his chest.

"Don't move!" Hayley said. "Stay really still and breathe."

Dylan cried harder.

I jumped into the mud to try to yank him out, but I sank past my knees. When I tried to move I sank farther, still a few yards from Dylan.

"Take this!" Hayley said.

She reached the metal detector to me, careful to stay on the bank. I tried to lift my left foot, and my shoe came off. I creeped forward enough to get the metal detector to Dylan's hands, but suddenly I was up to my waist in the quicksand.

"Grab it!" I yelled.

Dylan reached and pulled and the detector went under. He sank farther.

"Stop!" Hayley shouted. "Don't move any more or he'll go under." She hurried toward the road.

Dylan whimpered and tried to stand straight. I let the metal detector sink and moved slowly toward him, but the muck was so thick it sucked my right shoe and sock off.

My heart raced and I tried to calm down. "Why'd you come out here?" I said.

"I saw a shiny thing," he said. "Ashley, I'm sinking."

"Just stay still," I said.

The longer I was in the mud, the more desperate I felt. The stuff looked like the clay you play with in first grade, only it didn't smell good. I inched forward, sinking even more, until I could reach Dylan. He lunged, missed my hand, and sank farther. I made one last attempt and grabbed his hand. I pulled him up, but that made me sink to my armpits. Dylan came out without shoes, socks, or pants.

"Hang on, Ash!" Hayley said, running back toward us with yellow jumper cables. A young woman came over the hill behind her. As soon as she spotted us she said a bad word, and I knew we were in big trouble.

Hayley stood on the edge of the bank and threw one end of the cable to me. It slopped in the muck and I snatched it. "Get him out first," I yelled, wrapping the cable around Dylan's chest.

Hayley and the woman pulled him across the top of the mud, his little behind jiggling as he bounced along. If I hadn't thought I was about to die, it would have been funny.

I was so relieved when they pulled him onto the bank, but the mud was up to my chest now and pushing on my lungs. I could hardly breathe. I quit moving, quit trying to get a better foothold. I was slowly sinking.

Please, God. I don't want to die this way.

CHAPTER 24

☺ *Bryce* ☺

I was about to leave Jeff's house when the doorbell rang. It was Denise, one of our classmates. To say Ashley and I didn't get along with her is like saying David and Goliath weren't pals. She had lied about Ashley in band and had almost hurt her at an amusement park before the end of school.

"Oh," she said, glancing at the address on the house like she was at the wrong place.

I said I was just leaving and that the Alexanders weren't home.

"Well, could you put this in their fridge?" She handed me a casserole dish with foil on top. The thing weighed about 10 pounds.

She turned to leave, but I asked if she knew anything about Jeff's collection.

"Sure. Everybody's heard about it, but I've never actually seen it. Could I take a peek? I wouldn't tell anybody."

"Sorry," I said. "The room's locked, and I don't have a key. Maybe next time."

CHAPTER 25

Ashley

Hayley and the woman tossed me the jumper cables, but if they managed to pull me out, would the mud tear my clothes off as it had Dylan's? I was glad no one else was watching.

I grabbed the muddy cables, but when Hayley and the woman pulled, my hands kept slipping.

"Tie it around you!" the woman yelled.

I finally got it around me as the mud sneaked toward my shoulders. I kept praying as they tugged with all their might. At first nothing happened. Then the cable bit into my skin, and I inched forward. It felt like a vacuum cleaner was sucking me down. I wanted to hang on to my shorts, but I knew if I let go of the cable I'd sink.

Dylan clapped as they pulled me, and once I knew I was going to be safe, I saw his towel fall off and I laughed. Soon I was crying with relief as they dragged me across the mud like a wounded turtle.

Someone appeared at the top of the hill talking on a cell phone. A siren wailed in the distance.

As soon as I reached the shore, Hayley gripped my hands and helped me up. The woman threw me a towel. I draped it over me and sat next to Dylan, crying and exhausted.

The siren stopped, and a police officer rushed down the hill. The woman offered to give Dylan and me a ride, and I liked that idea a whole lot better than going home in a police car.

Before she pulled out, I heard the police officer saying something into his radio. I rolled down my window. "Tell the county we need a fence around this place," he said. "These two just about didn't make it."

That sent shivers down my spine. Then he added, "There's something under the water in the deep section of the lake. I think it's a car."

CHAPTER 26

☺ *Bryce* ☺

Ashley burst through the door carrying Dylan, both covered in mud.

"Looks like you guys had fun," I said.

She glared at me, then spilled the story. Boy, did I feel like an idiot.

"Get Dylan in the shower," she said, heading upstairs. "Then you and I need to get back to Hayley at the lake."

"Why?"

Ashley told me what the cop had said. "I have to see if this is Gunnar's Jeep and if he's in it."

A little later she came down with wet hair just as Leigh walked in.

She'd been looking for a summer job for a couple of weeks, and I could tell by her face she'd had no luck.

Ashley asked Leigh if she would watch Dylan until Mom got home, and Leigh agreed only after Ashley promised her twice as much as Mom was going to pay her for the whole day. Leigh may not be much of a sister, but you have to admire her business sense.

By the time we got to the lake, a tow truck had backed up to the edge of the hill and a guy in a wet suit was in the water. A few minutes later the truck pulled a yellow Jeep Cherokee from the muddy lake.

Hayley covered her mouth, and Ashley put an arm around her.

"That's his Jeep," Hayley said.

Grime covered the windshield. The policeman spoke to the tow-truck operator, and the man said it didn't look like the vehicle had been underwater that long. "Maybe a couple of weeks."

Others had gathered, and when the SUV was at the top of the hill, the officer asked everyone to stand back. Some pointed and whispered about Ashley being one of the stuck kids, and it made me want to leave, but we couldn't take our eyes off that yellow Jeep. Could Gunnar have plunged into the water? Was his body still in the SUV?

When the cop opened the door, water poured out, along with fish and crawdads.

"I can't stand this," Hayley said, stepping behind Ashley as if to keep from seeing something she didn't want to see.

The Jeep was full of mud and the seats were waterlogged, but I didn't see a body.

The officer opened the back. "Vehicle's clean," he said into his radio. "The plates match the missing person, but there's no one inside."

CHAPTER 27

✖ Ashley ✖

When Hayley told her aunt about the Jeep, the woman's eyes grew wide. She was relieved, of course, that Gunnar wasn't in the SUV. While we were there a reporter called for a newspaper story.

I dreaded going home. I knew I had to tell Mom what had happened at the lake. She had told me to keep a sharp eye on Dylan, and I had let her down. I kept giving Dylan more mashed potatoes and butter to keep him quiet during dinner. Afterward I helped Mom clear the table and start the dishes.

My plan was to not tell the story at all, but the longer I kept quiet, the harder that became. Mom had asked what I did all day, and when I didn't answer she turned from the sink and squinted. "I heard something on the news about a vehicle pulled from the lake today. You weren't part of that, were you?"

"Sort of," I said. At first the story was stuck as deep as Dylan and I were in the mud. Then I pulled it free, and the whole thing slid out.

Mom glanced at Dylan in the living room watching Thomas the Tank Engine. I could tell she was upset. Then she hugged me, and I cried like a gushing fire hydrant.

"Do you have to tell Sam?" I said, sobbing.

She pulled away and wiped my tears. That's about as close as any person can get to another. She was being more than my mom. She was also being my friend.

"I know how bad you feel," she said, hesitating. I was expecting her to add, "I'm really disappointed" or "I guess I can't trust you with Dylan anymore." Instead, she wiped her own eyes and said, "I think all you need to know right now is how much I love you."

Leigh came in and asked for her money. I thought Mom would stick up for me and try to get Leigh to lower her rate, since she was charging a fortune. But no.

Our dogs, Pippin and Frodo, followed Leigh and me to my room and kept sniffing at my legs. I had just enough money saved to buy a skirt I'd seen at the mall. I handed it over.

"Nice doing business with you," Leigh said, smiling.

☺ *Bryce* ☺

I was playing a video game in the barn when Jeff called. If the doctor said he couldn't go on the bike trip that meant he might be getting better. If he could go, I knew it would mean there was no reason for him to stay home, because he was dying.

I thought back to when he was first told he had a bad disease. *Malignancy*, they called it. None of us knew anything was wrong. He just started running funny in gym, wobbling to one side. We all laughed at him and called him Weeble because of an old toy. The commercial said, "Weebles wobble, but they don't fall down."

But Jeff did fall down, and I admit I laughed when Duncan Swift called him Spaz. Duncan and I regretted it later when we heard Jeff had cancer, but there's no way to take it back. It's almost like Jeff forgave us without saying anything.

"You won't believe it, Bryce," Jeff said, as excited as I'd ever heard him. "Not only did the doctor say I could go, but he's also donating five dollars a mile!"

CHAPTER 29

✖ Ashley ✖

The next day I was working on a jumble—a word with its letters all mixed up—and was stuck on the final one. The letters were: *seluc.* I asked Bryce to help.

The phone rang and it was Taryn, Gunnar's former girlfriend. "We talked the other day," she said.

"I remember."

"I saw the story in the paper about Gunnar's Jeep," she said. "I'm worried about him."

Join the club.

I told her we had been there when they pulled the SUV out and what I knew from Gunnar's mother, which wasn't much.

"One of the things we fought about when we were dating was his always going off and not telling anyone," she said. "He'd take a couple of days off work and just disappear, usually right after he got his paycheck. When he'd come back he'd complain about being broke. He never told me where the money went. I think that's why he lived with his mother. He never had enough to do anything but make his car payments."

I thanked her and told her I'd get the information to the right people.

Bryce smiled and grabbed my pencil. "Got it!" he said.

He scribbled *clues* in the jumble box.

CHAPTER 30

☺ *Bryce* ☺

Jeff gave me a tour of the van his parents had rented for the bike trip. It was longer than most and looked more like an RV. It had a sink, a bathroom, a long couch and table, DVD player, satellite TV—the works.

Jeff seemed in a bad mood. "I wanted to do this myself, you know," he said. "Camp out, ride the trails. They're going to follow us and treat us like kids. I know it's because they care, but it ticks me off."

I found Jeff's parents inside. Normally I don't like to bring stuff up to adults, whether they're teachers or parents. But this seemed different.

I explained what Jeff had told me and asked if there was anything they could do.

They looked at each other. "The doctor said he could go because he doesn't have much longer," Mrs. Alexander said. "We need to be there."

"But can you hang back?" I said. "Let us camp out and ride like the others?"

Jeff's dad nodded. "I suppose. But if he needs to stop, we'll be there."

CHAPTER 31

✖ Ashley ✖

A group of us waved good-bye to Jeff and his parents as they drove away, headed for Vail and a special camp. Bryce would join them Saturday morning.

Bryce rode his bike with weights on his legs and arms, and I rode beside him. We stopped at Jeff's house first and put small pieces of paper in the front and back doors, so if anyone went inside the paper would fall and we'd know it. We put another on the window to the trophy room and one on the garage door.

We hit the Santa Fe Trail, and by the time we passed the Air Force Academy, I could see how strong Bryce had grown. I huffed and puffed like a steam engine, while he was hardly sweating.

We stopped at a small covered booth to get out of the sun and have something to drink. Clouds drifted lazily over the valley. Over the mountain range was Pikes Peak, which Bryce would see a lot of in the next few days.

It was the first time we had talked about my fiasco in the mud. People say twins know everything about each other, that they can sense when the other is in danger or in pain. Sometimes Bryce doesn't even know I'm in pain when I'm standing right next to him screaming.

"Must have been pretty scary," he said.

I nodded. "Might be more scary for you the next few days with Jeff. I hope he makes it."

CHAPTER 32

JEFF'S DIARY

by Jeff Alexander

It's only a day before the bike trip of a lifetime, and I couldn't be more excited. A lot of people biking this year had cancer and beat it, so that gives me hope. There are also people biking who have lost someone they love to cancer.

I met Bob yesterday, whose daughter, Cassie, died just last year. You'd think he would not want to be around people like me, but he smiled and gave me a hug. He actually rode with Cassie last year in a specially made carrier that she sat in. He said he wouldn't trade that experience for anything.

He said being around Cassie and me makes him appreciate every moment of life, so I guess that's something we can all learn. He also believes nothing happens to us that surprises God. Not my cancer, not a car wreck, or even a terror attack. (I have a friend whose dad was killed in a plane crash caused by terrorists.)

Over the next few days we're supposed to go 200 miles and wind up in Colorado Springs. I'm hoping there will be some people there when we finish—though I'm kind of nervous. A lot of people riding in this have really strong legs and look like they've biked for years.

My doctor gave thumbs-up to this ride and even kicked in a bunch of money per mile. If you can contribute, that's great. If not, that's okay too. Just keep praying someone will find a cure.

When you read this, I'll be on the road and going through the most beautiful mountains God ever made!

CHAPTER 33

☺ *Bryce* ☺

I had a hard time getting to sleep Friday night and spent a couple of hours on the Internet checking eBay. I found some of the same memorabilia that had been stolen from Jeff, but it was from places like New York and North Carolina. And none of the signed stuff had Jeff's name on it.

In the morning Sam sipped his coffee, and we talked about baseball as he drove me to the bike-hike site. He had rooted for the Cincinnati Reds when he was a kid and now didn't seem to have a favorite. My team is the Cubs, even though I live in Colorado. I like the Rockies, but there's a loyalty I feel with my real dad. Some of the best times we ever had were watching the Cubs make some late-inning comeback. Plus, we were able to go to the "friendly confines" of Wrigley Field a few times.

"I talked with Jeff's mom and dad last night," Sam said, finally changing the subject as we drove through the Eisenhower tunnel. "They wanted to make sure you knew that you don't have to finish this."

"Not finishing would kill Jeff."

Sam pursed his lips, like that was a poor choice of words. "But in his condition, I'm not sure he's going to be able to help much. And the hills you're going to tackle are not like the ones on the Santa Fe Trail."

"We'll walk them if we have to."

Brake lights flashed ahead of us. Sam pulled into the left lane to pass a huge truck and muttered something. He pointed to the median where the body of a deer with a huge rack of antlers was tangled in the guardrail. There was blood on the road, and people slowed to look.

"Sam, did you ever have any friends die when you were a kid?"

He rubbed the stubble of his beard. "First grade. Kid in my class was helping his little brother cross the street. His brother got excited and broke away from him. The car wasn't going that fast, but I guess fast enough. They didn't have crisis counselors back then. Everybody just kind of went on without talking about it."

"It bothered you?"

"I was sad. I knew the kid, had played with him a few times. I still think about him. Wonder why it happened."

Sam's first wife and young daughter died too. Sometimes hard things draw people toward God while others are pushed away. Jeff had certainly gotten closer.

"Anyway," Sam said, "the Alexanders appreciate what you're doing. And I'm proud of you too."

CHAPTER 34

❀ Ashley ❀

Hayley and I walked to her aunt's house early. When we got there I saw a long, black car parked in front.

Hayley studied the car. "I don't recognize it. I don't think I have any relatives with a car like that."

The windows were tinted black, so we couldn't see inside. Hayley looked in one of the house windows near the porch. "Two guys are sitting in the living room talking to my aunt. She looks upset."

Someone cleared his throat behind us. I swung around to a huge guy in a shiny suit—he looked like a shark with sunglasses. His arms were like tree trunks and his chest was a barrel. He had dark eyebrows, black hair, and a neatly trimmed mustache.

"How are you today, ladies?" he said, smiling. "Can I help you?"

The only time I was called a lady was by a teacher when I was doing something wrong at school.

"Just checking on my aunt," Hayley said.

"Who are you?" I said.

The guy seemed surprised at the tone of my voice. "Friends of Gunnar. We're worried about him."

The other two came outside. They weren't as big as The Shark, but both looked like they had a million-dollar clothing allowance.

"Either of you seen Gunnar?" a short man said.

"Why?" I said before Hayley could answer.

The short man glared at me. "'Cause we wanna know."

"No," Hayley said. "How do you know him?"

The short one waved the other two toward the car.

We hurried inside.

CHAPTER 35

☺ *Bryce* ☺

I couldn't believe all the colorful outfits and smiling faces at the start of the race. Bikes looked like rainbows lined up behind yellow police tape that said Do Not Cross. Bikers wore Bike for the Cure T-shirts. The organizers handed out numbers to attach to our bikes.

Jeff's face lit up when he saw me. "Have I got a lot to tell you!"

"Save it for the hike," I said, smiling. "We'll have plenty of time to talk out there."

Jeff's phone chirped. I figured it was someone from the newspaper or maybe a friend, but he talked a long time at the back of the van. I tried to listen in, but he was too far away. When Jeff returned I asked who was on the phone.

"Nobody." He turned. "Hey, Mr. Timberline, you going to take over if Bryce gets tired?"

Sam shook his head. "They'll have to drag him off that bike before I can take over."

Finally it was time to mount up. I couldn't wait.

CHAPTER 36

❀ Ashley ❀

Hayley's aunt's face was puffy and red.

"What did those guys want?" Hayley said.

"Gunnar. They wouldn't stop asking questions, as if I knew something and didn't want to tell them."

"Were they the police?" Hayley said.

I knew they weren't. At least, they didn't look like any police officers I'd ever seen.

Hayley's aunt shook her head. "They wanted to go through his apartment, but I said no."

"Were they friends of his?" I said.

"That's what they said, but I've never seen them before."

I hurried to the window to write down their license-plate number, but they were already gone. I kicked myself for not thinking of it earlier.

Hayley's aunt wrung her hands. "They saw the article in the newspaper. They've been looking for Gunnar a long time."

"Did they know him from work?" I said.

She shrugged, trembling. "I think Gunnar is in trouble."

CHAPTER 37

☺ *Bryce* ☺

I liked that we weren't racing. Not that I don't like competition, but everyone was riding against cancer and with each other.

One of the Colorado Springs television stations sent their news truck and taped the start. The reporter, a nice-looking woman with short red hair, leaned down to ask Jeff some questions.

When she finished we put on our helmets and checked the microphones. Jeff's mom and dad took pictures as we got into position. Someone fired a starter gun, and we all whooped and hollered as we took off.

Riding with the wind in our faces, going downhill, was the best.

We'd waited for this for weeks, and Jeff had been planning it for months.

The first few miles were paved as part of a bike track. We started in the middle of the pack and coasted. People around us gave Jeff high fives.

Jeff's voice came over the speakers in my helmet crystal clear. "We're actually doing this, Timberline. Can you believe it?"

"You're gonna believe it the first time we have to go uphill," I said.

"I could ride a thousand hills today."

Jeff sounded pumped, but his skin was pale and his eyes droopy. We were also at a high elevation, so there was less oxygen than we were used to.

The Alexanders drove slowly past us, shooting us with their video camera. Sam drove behind them and waved just before he turned around. There was something lonely about not having family with you but also something exciting. It was the summer adventure I'd been waiting for.

I just hoped Jeff and I would finish this race together.

CHAPTER 38

❈ Ashley ❈

Instead of heading straight home, I went to Johnny's Pawn and Deli. People bring stuff in there to sell all the time, and I wondered if the owner had seen any of Jeff's things.

The owner is a round man with a bizarre-looking beard. Part of it is tied with rubber bands. He also has tattoos of snakes crawling up both arms.

I showed him the list of stolen stuff. "I wish I had even one of these," he said, shaking his head. "Good, expensive stuff."

"It was all actually stolen from a friend of mine. He has cancer."

The man clenched his teeth, and his jaw muscles flexed underneath the beard. "The kid that's in the paper?"

I nodded.

He picked up a phone. "Hang on a minute."

While he talked I moseyed around his store, which carried everything from used saxophones to chain saws. He also sold guns and jewelry, and Mrs. Watson said he made the best turkey-and-ham sub in town.

"I checked a couple of stores in the Springs," he said. "We'll all be on the lookout for this stuff."

I passed our middle school on the way back to my ATV. I was looking forward to being one of the oldest kids in school for a change.

A concrete truck peeked out from the back of the building. A huge tarp stretched behind it, so I moved closer to see what was going on.

A guy wearing a hard hat was drinking coffee out of a thermos and sitting on a light pole. He waved. "Can't go back there."

"What are you building?"

"Can't say. Just stay away, okay?"

CHAPTER 39

☺ *Bryce* ☺

The first four miles were easy. A stream ran by the bike trail, and it was a strange mix to hear water lapping over rocks and the *click-click* of bike chains, pedals, and tires on pavement.

I glanced back at Jeff. He looked tired but was still smiling as riders passed and waved.

"You okay?" I said.

He panted like a spent dog. "Couldn't be better."

As we neared an incline we talked about lunch, where we might camp that night, and what DVD to watch in his parents' van.

"I don't want anything to do with the van," Jeff said.

I thought I'd better change the subject. "Anybody ever ask you about all the stuff in your trophy room?"

He chuckled. "It's funny. I don't like sports that much. And I haven't seen any movies of most of the stars who sent pictures."

"How'd they find out about you?"

"Probably got my name on some list. Don't get me wrong. I appreciate the thoughts, but the thing that means the most to me is the letter I got from the president."

"I'd like to see that," I said.

"It's in the glass case. I wrote and told him I'd prayed for him and mentioned I was going through treatment for cancer. He sent a handwritten letter back and said he was moved by what I had written. He told me he would pray for me during our bike ride and even pledged some money."

"Wow!"

"Yeah, I'm hoping to keep that letter a long time."

CHAPTER 40

�֎ Ashley ✖

Bryce beeped me from the trail while they were on a 10-minute rest. I had asked Mom if I could keep her cell phone to stay in touch with him, and she said I could. I wanted to tell Bryce about the guys at Hayley's aunt's place, but he seemed in a hurry.

"I need a favor," he whispered. "Get Sam's binoculars and go over to Jeff's house."

"Why binoculars?"

"I need you to look in the trophy room and see if there's a framed, handwritten letter from the president. I'll call you later."

I rode my ATV to Jeff's house. Little flags stuck in the yard said things like "Good luck, Jeff" and "You go, boy!" I checked the doors and windows and found our pieces of paper still in place.

The window to the trophy room was too high off the ground for me to see inside. The only thing that would put me high enough was a picnic table a few yards away. It took a few minutes to edge it close enough, but I didn't need the binoculars. The glass case was empty except for one thing in the back corner. In fact, the whole room was empty. Nothing on the walls. Nothing on top of the case.

CHAPTER 41

☺ *Bryce* ☺

After the first four miles, the riding got really hard. It made me wonder who had chosen the route—it almost felt like someone was trying to punish us.

I rode with my head down, trying to focus on putting one foot in front of the other, and when I looked up, the sight took my breath away. Mountains rose on our right and left with trees so thick you couldn't tell one from another.

"Makes you feel pretty small, huh?" Jeff said, trying to catch his breath. He was working hard to keep up his end of the pedaling.

We wound around a hill, always going up. The only thing between us and the edge was a guardrail. Others didn't seem to struggle, but Jeff and I were going so slow it was hard to keep the bike upright.

The Alexanders pulled up beside us. "Why don't you get in and we'll drive you to the top?" Jeff's mom said.

Jeff waved her off and pedaled harder. The bike lurched as he grunted and strained.

"Easy, big boy," I said.

"Parents," Jeff said.

By lunch we had gone up and down several hills. The leader and most experienced cyclist was a man named Gary. He was thin and wiry, and the muscles in his legs looked like ropes.

"The next part is probably the toughest climb, outside of the long ascent to Woodland Park," he said. "Everybody feeling okay?"

Most shouted, "Yeah," but I felt too tired to say anything. Jeff stared at his parents, still watching from their van.

CHAPTER 42

❀ Ashley ❀

Bryce said he was on a bathroom break when he called. When I told him what I had seen at Jeff's house, he couldn't believe it.

"Ash, I just looked in there a couple of days ago. There was still a lot of stuff left."

"Well, it's gone now."

"Then why weren't the pieces of paper disturbed?" he said.

"Must be some other way in," I said. "You want me to call the police?"

"Not yet."

I told him about the men Hayley and I had run into at her aunt's house.

"Call Gunnar's boss," he said. "He might know these guys."

It felt odd being separated from Bryce, trying to solve two mysteries at once.

CHAPTER 43

⊙ *Bryce* ⊙

That afternoon was the longest of my life. With the sun beating down I could hardly think about the beautiful scenery. I might as well have been biking through a desert or some hallway with no windows.

Jeff spoke into a digital recorder, recording thoughts he could include in his next article.

We went through a small town called Minturn, where there was a gas station with American flags flying and a general store. The houses looked like they'd been stuck there between the mountains by God himself.

A sign told us we were going through the San Isabel National Forest. Clouds cast shadows on the mountains on both sides, moving across the landscape like slow trains. I wished I could get on one and ride it to the end of our trip.

"You sure you don't want to take your parents up on that ride in the van?" I said.

"Keep pedaling," Jeff said.

With aspens to our right and pine trees to our left, we headed up again. We passed a lake we had seen from Sam's flyover. People sat on the shore fishing.

"Man, I'd like to do that someday," Jeff said.

"I'd like to do that right now."

We rode up one hill and saw a sign that said we were traveling the Tenth Mountain Division Memorial Highway. I remembered something about it from reading about World War II. The tenth was an elite division trained on ski slopes in Colorado to go into Europe and hunt down the bad guys. I wondered if their legs had felt like spaghetti like mine.

We made it to the top of the last hill for the day and rode into Leadville. On a map, it doesn't look that far from Vail, less than 40 miles, but this trip has taught me never to trust a map. My back felt like it would snap any minute, and my legs cramped. Others around us raised their fists.

The leader, Gary, rode alongside Jeff and me as we hit the town. "Didn't think you two were going to make it. Tomorrow's going to be easier."

That felt like an answer to prayer.

CHAPTER 44

✖ Ashley ✖

Hayley told me where Gunnar worked. I called just before clos-
ing and asked for his manager.

"You got him."

I described the three men Hayley and I had met at her aunt's.

"Not anybody who works here," he said.

"Gunnar seem nervous about anything the last few days he was
there?"

"Like I told the police, he did seem jumpy. The phone would ring
or somebody would walk in the office and he'd get skittish. He just
said he wasn't feeling well."

"Anything else?"

"Nothing unusual. 'Cept he was always asking for an advance on his paycheck, but I wouldn't give it to him. I don't understand it. He always wore old clothes. I don't think he paid rent to his mother. Only thing he spent money on was his car payment. What'd he need money for?"

CHAPTER 45

☺ *Bryce* ☺

We rode through Leadville to curious stares along the main street. We passed old brick buildings, gift shops, a bank, and even an antique mall. Colorado Mountain College nearby specialized in teaching about the outdoors.

Houses in town seemed old and some were leaning. A little hotel made me think the Hilton family didn't have anything to worry about. Signs pointed to a mining museum, and others advertised mountain property.

Jeff and I turned into a campground and found lots of tents and people gathered around picnic tables. We were the last to arrive, and people clapped as we pulled to a stop.

We ate with Jeff's parents, gazing at Mount Elbert to the west. The Arkansas River was not far away, and I heard we would be riding by it the next day.

Mrs. Alexander kept asking Jeff to sleep in the van, and he finally walked away in a huff.

"Did you move the rest of the stuff from the trophy room?" I said when he was gone.

"We didn't move anything," Mr. Alexander said. "Why?"

I told him what Ashley had seen.

"She must have been looking in the wrong room," Mrs. Alexander said. "We have another glass cabinet in an empty room."

That was a relief.

I found Jeff in our tent, fuming and trying to get his sleeping bag unrolled.

"I can't believe they're following us," he said. "I wish they'd just go away."

I pressed my lips together, trying to keep quiet. But I couldn't. "Why don't you lay off your parents?" I yelled. "They're just trying to help."

CHAPTER 46

✽ Ashley ✽

I called Taryn, Gunnar's ex-girlfriend, and left a message on her answering machine to call me.

Randy, Leigh's boyfriend, was over for dinner.

"My mom's been reading the articles in the paper about Jeff," Randy said. "I feel sorry for him, but he sure seems to have a strong faith."

Leigh sighed.

Mom looked at her. "You don't think his faith is helping him?"

"I don't want to rag on the kid," Leigh said, "but he's probably parroting stuff he's heard from his parents."

I put my fork down and wiped my mouth. "I've been there when he writes his column. He doesn't even pass it by his mom before he sends it to the paper."

"I'm just saying some of the stuff is probably from a sermon he's heard."

Mom's face turned red, and it was her turn to put her fork down, but she kept quiet.

Sam looked back and forth between Leigh and Mom, then asked Dylan to pass the mashed potatoes. If I hadn't taken them from him, they would have landed in the green beans.

Randy broke the silence. "I don't know. I think the kid's working out what he thinks about God in the middle of something really scary. Gotta admire that."

"I'm sure thinking about God taking him to heaven will comfort him," Leigh said. "I just don't think it's true."

"Why not?" Randy said.

"God's supposed to love everybody. Why would he give cancer to a kid? Why would he let those kids die the other day in the trailer fire we saw on the news? Or a mom and her daughter in a plane crash?"

That shut everyone up. Dylan looked at us like there was a bomb under the table, and to be honest, it felt like it.

Leigh finally put her napkin on the table and went to her room.

"I didn't mean to upset anybody," Randy said.

"Not your fault," Sam drawled. "Truth is, there's a lot more going on than you know."

CHAPTER 47

☺ *Bryce* ☺

Here I'd asked God to make me a good friend to Jeff, and now I'd yelled at him and blown it.

"Sorry," I said, "I shouldn't have said that."

"No, no, don't be sorry. Be angry all you want." He sat up. "You know how long it's been since anybody got mad enough at me to be honest?"

"I don't understand."

"My parents, teachers, everybody tries to be so careful. Drives me crazy. I can be a jerk, but everybody's feeling so sorry for me that they don't say anything. You don't know how good it feels to have someone actually get mad."

"You should spend more time around Ashley," I said, and we both laughed.

Jeff sighed. "People try to keep stuff from you when they should just go ahead and say it. Like, I know why the doctor said I could go on this ride. He doesn't think I have much longer, but would he or anybody else tell me that? No."

I felt bad for keeping the trophy room secret from him, but I had promised his parents. He talked about school, people at church, and friends who talked down to him, like having cancer meant he couldn't think anymore.

"Know what?" he said. "The one I'm really mad at is God. I try not to, but the truth is, when you boil it down, he let me get cancer."

"Humph," I said. "I always thought that God must trust you a lot to let you go through this."

Jeff flinched. "What do you mean?"

"Well, he knew you believed in him. He must have known how you would react. He trusted you to go through it."

Jeff frowned. "That's a thought. He's the one giving me the strength. That's funny. I'm mad at the one giving me strength."

I hadn't meant to be profound. It just slipped out.

CHAPTER 48

✖ Ashley ✖

I'd been praying for Leigh for a long time. She'd been upset about her mom and little sister dying, and I knew she blamed God, even though she said she didn't believe he even existed. I left the table and went up to her room, which was like walking into a lion's den—a lion who didn't make her bed and was painting her toenails.

She rolled her eyes. "You're not going to make this any better."

"I just wanted to apologize," I said. "I didn't mean to make you mad."

She shrugged and kept painting. "It's not just you. Everybody's buying into God these days. Taking the easy way out."

"The easy way out?"

"God's a crutch. You don't have to deal with problems—you put them on God. If things go bad, it was his plan. He's up there pulling the strings and we're puppets. Does that offend you?"

"No, because I know you feel bad. And I'm guessing that Jeff's cancer gets to you just like it does the rest of us."

She sat on her bed. "How long have you known him?"

"Since we moved here." I told her all the stories I knew, about how people laughed at him in gym class and how shocked we were when we heard the news.

"Is he going to die?" Leigh said.

I shook my head. "I don't know, but I don't want to keep fighting with you about God. I mean, I want you to believe, but I don't think it's good for us to be mad at each other."

"Fine, but don't waste your time," she said. "I'll never believe like you, so don't get your hopes up."

CHAPTER 49

☻ *Bryce* ☻

I was on the bike, near the edge of a canyon. The front wheel kept getting close to the edge of the drop-off, and there was no guardrail. The front tire kicked little pebbles over the side, and they bounced into the bottomless chasm.

A huge black bird flew beside me, looking me in the eye and cawing. Its wings brushed the front tire that got caught in a rut. If I didn't get out, we'd plunge over the edge.

I looked back, but Jeff wasn't there. I screamed, echoing off the canyon walls. I looked for other riders, but I was alone.

The rut swerved right, and my front tire went to the edge.

I slammed on the brakes, but the pedals spun. I grabbed for handlebar brakes that weren't there.

As the front tire left the pavement, I screamed again. The bike went out from under me, and I felt weightless, falling into the abyss.

"Bryce!" someone yelled. It was Jeff, calling me in my helmet.

I sat up straight in the tent. Jeff shook my shoulder. My legs trembled, and I wiped sweat from my forehead.

Jeff smirked. "Dreaming about Marion Quidley?"

"Wasn't that bad. Just going over a cliff and falling to my death."

"Did you hit bottom? I've heard you never actually hit bottom in those dreams. And if you do, it means you're dead."

"You woke me just in time."

He picked up his digital recorder and punched Play. It was me moaning and groaning. Jeff laughed and I snatched it from him. He tried to grab it back, but I held it until I could erase my voice.

"What'd you do that for!?" he yelled.

"Serves you right for recording me," I said. "Remember, no special preferences for people with cancer."

He smiled, laid back on his sleeping bag, and opened the net above us so we could see the sky. There wasn't much light from the nearby town, so it seemed we could see millions of stars.

"Tell me a secret," Jeff said. "You can trust me."

"Only if you tell me one."

"Okay, but you have to promise that it stays right here."

"Deal."

Jeff searched for words. "I . . . I really like your sister."

"Seriously?"

"Yeah. She's pretty. Smart. And I love the way her hair smells."

I laughed and Jeff socked me on the shoulder so hard I knew I'd have a bruise. "How would you know how her hair smells?"

"I sat behind her in second period. If she doesn't dry her hair before school it takes that long to dry out. I think she uses Pert."

I shook my head. "You and Skeeter are the only two who have a thing for her."

"I didn't say I was going to marry her or anything. It's just that she's the kind of girl I'd want to take to a movie or on a date when I grow up."

"Well, I never thought I'd say this, but I hope you get to take her out sometime."

"Okay, your turn."

I thought hard. I didn't have that many secrets, but two huge ones went through my mind.

"All right, but you have to swear—"

"You got it."

"Remember the story a few months ago about the thieves up at Gold Camp Road?"

"Yeah, and a car that went into the water."

"That was us—Ashley, Dylan, Sam, and me. We cracked the case."

"You're kidding! I knew you and Ashley liked to solve mysteries, but I never dreamed . . . Your secret's a lot better than mine. Why can't you tell anybody?"

"Long story," I said. "It has something to do with Sam and what he used to do. I'd tell you more, but I promised I wouldn't."

He yawned. "It's okay." He seemed weaker now and pale in the moonlight.

We lay there, staring at the sky, for a long time.

CHAPTER 50

✖ Ashley ✖

I was almost asleep when the phone rang.

"Sorry to call so late," Taryn said. "You wanted to talk?"

"Thanks," I said. "I'm wondering if Gunnar ever mentioned money problems."

"All the time. That was one of the things we fought about."

"Maybe he made some big purchase. Like an engagement ring."

"If he bought a ring, it was a mystery to me."

"But wouldn't that explain it? He wanted to marry you, and when you broke up with him, he couldn't take it. He pushed his Jeep in the lake and . . ."

"And what?" she said. "They haven't found his body, have they?"

"No."

"Then he pushed his Jeep in the lake and ran away? That makes no sense." She paused. "Look, I don't want to be mean, but I don't want you to call here anymore. I know you're trying to help, but I'd rather you leave me alone."

CHAPTER 51

◯ *Bryce* ◯

I hit the light button on my watch and saw it was 3 a.m.
Only 10 minutes had gone by since I had checked. I knew I'd be
worthless on the bike with no sleep. Jeff's heavy breathing didn't
make it any easier.

I wanted something to eat—maybe that would help—but the
leader had made us put all our food in airtight bags and store them in
the trunk of a car. I guess he was scared of bears.

I looked through the opening in the tent, hoping to see a star
streak across the sky. That happens all the time in the movies, and I
hear it happens a lot in Colorado, but I've never seen one.

I heard a car in the distance. Something rustled in the pine needles a few feet away. A twig snapped. Maybe big animals making small sounds.

Who could have stolen Jeff's stuff? I tried to bore myself to sleep by running through all the possibilities. Was it possible Gunnar's disappearance and the missing items were linked? What were the odds?

I had a lot more questions than answers, but I've found it's best to just let your mind run. What if Gunnar's mother was covering for him? What if the goons who showed up at her house bought sports items? Maybe Gunnar had sold them something fake.

Something crackled outside the tent, and I looked at my watch. 3:10. I scooted down in my sleeping bag and imagined Pippin and Frodo were with me.

Next thing I knew, Jeff was hovering over me with a big smile. "Time to wake up, bed head."

I could feel my hair sticking straight up, and I couldn't wait to get my helmet on.

By 8:00, we were on the road, pedaling away from Leadville. My legs and back were sore, but as soon as I got on the bike I found myself in rhythm with Jeff, who seemed stronger.

CHAPTER 52

❀ Ashley ❀

I awoke early and rode to Jeff's house, eager to find out if I'd had the wrong room all along. I found both rooms with glass cases, and both were empty.

I was about to get back on my ATV when a garage door opened across the street and a man wearing a suit and tie walked out to retrieve his Sunday paper.

"Heard anything about the bike trip?" he said. He must have recognized me from the send-off.

I told him what I knew. "Have you noticed anything funny at the house the past few days?"

"I've been away, but you can talk with my wife."

He took me inside and introduced me to her. She was having coffee and grabbed the newspaper from him when he came inside. I thought the guy might be going to church, but he said he was off to work. When he left, she offered me breakfast.

"Thanks, but I already ate. I don't want to take much of your time. I was just wondering if you'd noticed anything at the Alexanders' house."

She squinted. "As a matter of fact, there was a truck outside yesterday morning. Real early. A blue pickup. Had one of those toolbox things in the back."

"Did you see anybody?"

"A guy in a hard hat went to the door, but of course no one was home. He carried something back to his truck, a big armload of stuff."

CHAPTER 53

☺ *Bryce* ☺

The road from Leadville eventually ran by the Arkansas River. The riding wasn't as hard as the previous day, but as the sun rose, it got hotter. We had to take several breaks to rest and drink water.

Ashley beeped my phone, and I called her back when we took a break. She told me what she had found at Jeff's house. I covered the phone and asked Jeff if anyone was working on his house.

"My dad had some work done on our roof a few weeks ago," Jeff said. "Why?"

"Ashley says a construction guy was at your house yesterday."

"What was she doing at our house?"

I told Ashley I'd get back to her and hung up.

Jeff faced me, his face tight. "What's going on?"

I didn't want to lie, but I also didn't want to betray his parents or get him upset.

The leader, Gary, blew his whistle and told us it was time to mount up.

"Come on," I said.

"Tell me or I'm not getting on the bike."

I sighed. "Can't Ashley keep an eye on your house while you're gone? I'd think you'd appreciate that."

He looked at the ground and shook his head as he climbed on. "Something's fishy."

CHAPTER 54

Ashley

Hayley wanted to stay away, but I talked her into going to her aunt's house. I asked her aunt if we could see Gunnar's apartment again. "If you think it might help," she said.

She gave us the key, and we went outside and climbed the stairs. The wood by the doorknob was splintered, and the door stood open a few inches.

"Think they could still be in there?" Hayley whispered.

"They probably came last night," I said, but I pushed the door slowly and peeked in. The mattress was off the bed, and the dresser drawers had been dumped on the floor. The closet had been rifled, and the little desk in the corner was a mess too.

I went to the computer monitor and hit the Power button. The screen flickered, but nothing came on. I tapped the keys. Still nothing.

"Ashley, it's gone," Hayley said, pointing at the floor.

The cables connecting the computer tower to the monitor and keyboard lay on the floor.

"Call the police," I said.

CHAPTER 55

☺ *Bryce* ☺

Jeff and I passed several blue Adopt a Highway litter-control signs. Other signs advertised horseback riding and property for sale. Another said Support Our Troops! The 14,000-foot mountains near Buena Vista, instead of being covered with trees, seemed to have had a buzz cut. Clouds cast huge shadows along the landscape.

A small plane passed overhead. Sam was supposed to be on a trip, but I wondered if he had detoured to fly over our group. The plane descended and circled, then flew so close to the ground that it took my breath away. As it passed, the pilot dipped its wing, and I saw the familiar numbers on the side. Sam actually gave me a thumbs-up.

"Hey!" Jeff said through the speaker in my helmet. "Isn't that the plane we were on?"

I had goose bumps. "Yep," I said. "That's my stepdad."

We went through Buena Vista, a small town with real elk walking around in it. People lined the streets, clapping and waving flags. Jeff's parents had driven ahead and were waiting with their video camera. Signs at restaurants advertised ice cream and root-beer floats, and I hoped we could come back later.

We followed our leader right and rode toward the hills, then left onto a dirt road. A few riders had dropped out, some with bike trouble, others had become sick. The rest of us bunched together, filling the road. People crowded around Jeff and me, encouraging us and patting us on the back.

We rode up a steep driveway to a camp run by a Christian group. At the top the driveway went straight down, and we had to ride our brakes. The cafeteria was a log cabin, and there was a nice gift shop across the grounds where I hoped to find a shirt for Ashley and something fun for Dylan. There was a basketball court, but people were so tired they went to the log cabin above the courtyard for our meeting.

There Gary congratulated us all for our determination. "We've gone almost halfway. We'll rest here and start off again late tomorrow morning."

Gary invited everyone back for a movie after dinner, and I was all for it until we got our room assignments. "Have a little surprise for you and Jeff," Gary said. "You two are headed over the hill for some intense R & R."

I wasn't sure I liked the word *intense*. Sounded like rock climbing or something.

CHAPTER 56

✖ Ashley ✖

"We can't call the police," Hayley's aunt said. She looked like a deer caught in headlights. "I didn't tell you everything those guys said. They told me if I went to the police, I'd never see Gunnar alive again."

Hayley gasped.

"His Jeep was found in the lake," she continued. "I suppose those guys did it."

"But they don't know where he is," I said. "How can they hurt him if—?"

"I'm not going to the police," she said.

On my way home, I passed the middle school. The tarp was still on the outside, and a wood saw whined. Another cement truck sat near a few construction trucks. One was a blue pickup with a tool-box in the bed.

I peeked inside the cab and saw a box on the front seat. I stepped up on the running board to get a better look.

"What are you doing?" someone said. I turned to see a man with massive sweat stains on his T-shirt. He had dark hair and a scar on his forehead.

My legs shook. "I go to school here."

"In my truck?"

I pointed. "No, at the school."

"Then why are you trying to get in my truck?"

"Oh! I wasn't. I was just—one of my friends has some things missing. Mind telling me what's in that box?"

He stepped closer. "If I were you, I'd leave right now."

I took his advice, but I looked back and got his license-plate number. He was still staring at me.

CHAPTER 57

☺ *Bryce* ☺

We rode in Jeff's parents' van on a dirt road around the mountain. The setting sun cast a golden glow, the river a brown snake winding through the valley. Homes perched on the side of the mountain seemed as if they might fall off at any moment. What must it be like to live here and watch the sun come up every morning or see clouds roll in and dump snow?

Jeff pointed at a swimming pool with a curly slide. Kids laughed and threw beach balls. On the other side of the road sat a general store with a couple of gas pumps. Behind that was a lodge where Gary waved us over to the edge of the parking lot.

A stream ran past it, and two more swimming pools lay at the bottom of the hill. "You two are staying here tonight. You can eat at the lodge restaurant and go swimming or just relax in the stream."

"Isn't it cold?" Jeff said.

Gary laughed. "Stick your foot in and find out. People come here in the winter in their bathing suits to sit in that hot springwater. In some places it's 130 degrees."

We unloaded our stuff and put it in front of the lodge door, then got the key at the front desk and said our good-byes to the Alexanders and Gary.

Jeff turned, his eyes bulging, and slapped me a high five. "Can you believe it? We've got this place to ourselves!"

After we put our stuff inside—where we found two beds, a TV, and a bathroom—we headed to the restaurant. It had a huge fireplace with a deer head and a moose head mounted over it, both complete with gigantic antlers. Standing taller than me was a stuffed bear, but the scariest thing was a stuffed mountain lion, poised to kill with its teeth bared. The eyes seemed to look right through you.

I had heard mountain lion screams near our house. They sound like humans, a haunting yell like a woman crying. Even though the thing was dead, it gave me the creeps. I couldn't imagine meeting one of those along the trail and having to defend myself.

Jeff ordered a buffalo burger, and I had grilled cheese. Then all I wanted was to soothe my sore muscles in that hot water.

CHAPTER 58

✽ Ashley ✽

I called everybody I could think of, even the principal's wife, but nobody knew anything about the building project at the school.

"Saw your brother today," Sam said that night. "Got close enough to see the smile on his face."

I wished I could have been there. *The Gazette* pictured the bicyclists arriving in Buena Vista and added that another report from Jeff and an in-depth story would follow the next day.

Mom said a group from the middle school was planning to meet the riders when they finished the trip.

I followed Sam to his office. I pulled a Post-it note from his stack and wrote down the license-plate number of the truck.

"What's this?" he said.

"I'm trying to find out who owns this truck. It's a suspicious vehicle."

Bryce and I tried not to ask Sam for help, but I knew he had contacts with the police.

He handed me a business card. "You've met this officer before. I don't think he'll give you information, but you can try."

CHAPTER 59

○ *Bryce* ○

The water felt so warm and good that when we started throwing a beach ball around, I almost forgot Jeff had cancer. We were just two kids having fun.

Later we walked down some steps to a concrete walkway. The river running past the pools was filled with rocks, many arranged in circles.

We scooted down the edge, hopping from rock to rock. I dipped a toe in one pool and pulled it back quickly. The water felt like it was boiling.

"Try this one!" Jeff said.

It was cooler. A few feet away the river was frigid, but here the water was toasty. A cool breeze blew, and goose bumps rose on my arms. A wave of warmth swept over me, and I realized the water was bubbling from beneath us rather than flowing from the river.

"I heard Native Americans used to come to these pools because they felt the water would heal their diseases," Jeff said.

"Yeah, they probably stopped here on those long bike trips hunting buffalo."

I closed my eyes and put my head back against a smooth rock, and it felt like I was floating on warmed air. The curve of the rock fit my head and neck perfectly. "I wish I could take this pool home with me, complete with the rocks and sand."

When Jeff didn't answer I opened my eyes and saw him staring across the stream. His mouth was open, and I was afraid he was having some sort of seizure.

"What's wrong?" I said, rolling over and splashing water on him.

He pointed. "Look under that rock over there."

There were pine trees and several large rocks on the other side. Something was moving under one of the rocks. It looked like a long band of diamonds against a yellow background.

"Looks like a bull snake!" someone downriver called.

I didn't care if it was a bull snake, a cow snake, or any other kind. I was done with the pool.

"I have to write my column," Jeff said.

We grabbed our stuff and headed back.

CHAPTER 60

✖ Ashley ✖

I struck out with the cop, but Mom knew a social worker—Liesel Parrish—who investigates kids in trouble or families who abuse children. I remembered she once said she could run the license-plate number of someone she was investigating, so I called her.

"Why do you want the info?" Liesel said.

I told her the owner of the truck was a construction guy working near our school. "I think he might have taken some stuff from my friend's house."

"Hmm," she said. "If you promise you'll contact the police if you find out anything and if you promise not to do anything dangerous, I'll e-mail you the information."

CHAPTER 61

JEFF'S DIARY

by Jeff Alexander

A 200-mile bike ride is a lot like having cancer. You're never sure what the next day will bring. With a disease, you can lose your hair, go through surgery, feel fine, or get dizzy and fall a lot. With a bike ride, the road could be bumpy or smooth. The clouds could roll in and you can't see much, or it can clear up and feel like you can see for a hundred miles. Or you can get dizzy and fall a lot.

I wouldn't want to go through cancer or a long bike ride without good friends. I'm riding with my friend Bryce. We're camping out, eating lunch, and even going in the hot springs together. It's sure made the difficult journey easier.

This morning I talked with our leader, Gary. His daughter died of cancer when she was five. He rides with a picture of her taped to his handlebars. I imagine she keeps him going mile after mile.

Gary keeps us going because he's always there in front, telling us where to go, what to do, and which trail to take. That reminds me of another friend who's good to have with you when you have a disease or even when you don't. A lot of people think God is a lucky charm you wear around your neck for good luck, or that he's some old guy in heaven just waiting to smack you when you do something wrong. But I've come to know Jesus as a friend who sticks closer than a brother. Even when I'm upset about my disease and want to blame God, Jesus is there.

The Bible says, "Do not be afraid or discouraged, for the Lord will personally go ahead of you. He will be with you; he will neither fail you nor abandon you."

It doesn't say he will heal you or take you out of something scary, but if you'll let him, Jesus will guide you through anything.

If you have pledged money to support our ride and for cancer research, thank you. I hope you'll be there when we finish in a couple of days.

CHAPTER 62

☺ *Bryce* ☺

The next morning we ate breakfast in the lodge with the mountain lion staring at us. Then Jeff and I stayed in the hot pool until his parents showed up. I didn't want to go near the water where Jeff and I had seen the snake, and I was glad he didn't bring it up. If Ashley had been here I'd have tried to get her to go, because she's spooked by anything that slithers. But the truth is, I'm just as afraid as she is.

As we packed, Jeff got a phone call and went outside to talk. When he came back we headed to the camp for a late-morning meeting. A storm was brewing. Gary talked with a TV weather guy and finally gave us the go-ahead.

The first mile was the hardest, trying to get back into the rhythm of pedaling together. The hot spring had loosened our muscles, but I wondered if the water had relaxed us too much. Jeff seemed slow, and he still looked pale.

Our goal was the bottom of Wilkerson Pass, but when we got within 10 miles of it, passing through Hartsel—population 75 with a gas station, a general store, and two restaurants—the clouds rolled in.

Buffalo and cattle grazed in a nearby field. I told Jeff we should play "Hey, Buffalo," where you holler at the animals and get a point for every one that actually looks up. I tried to scream, "Hey, Buffalo!" But I was so winded and tired I couldn't make them hear me.

I glanced back to see Jeff smile. He didn't even try my game.

Lightning struck on the horizon, and thunder rumbled soon after.

CHAPTER 63

✖ Ashley ✖

I slept late, then went downstairs and had breakfast at the computer. I found a message from Liesel Parrish.

```
Here's the information you wanted. FYI,
this guy looks clean. No arrests, warrants,
tickets. Remember, you promised you'd be
careful with this.
```

At the bottom she listed his name, Clarke Jeppeson, and his work and home phone numbers. I called his office and reached a secretary. I told her I was a student at Red Rock Middle School and had noticed construction there. "Can you tell me what's going on?"

I heard her rattle some papers. "Here's a number you can call."

"So you don't know what's going on?" I said.

"Clarke told me to give that number to anyone who calls. Okay?"

I dialed but reached the voice mail of someone who identified himself as Tim Minaro at DM.

I hung up before the beep, wondering what DM stood for.

CHAPTER 64

☺ *Bryce* ☺

The longer we rode, the cloudier it got. The sky looked like a sheet of foam with the little nubs sticking out. It was pretty, and I'd never seen it like that before, but frankly I'd rather have seen it from inside a nice warm house or car.

Every time lightning flashed, Jeff gasped. I asked if he wanted to pull over, but he said he wanted to keep up with the others.

"Know what I do when I get scared?" he said, huffing and puffing. "I make up jokes."

"Okay," I said.

"What did the little kid on the trail say to the mountain lion?"

I chuckled. "I give up."

"'I hope you're stuffed.'"

It was bad, but it took my mind off the lightning. Then it was back and forth, trying to make each other laugh. "What did the buffalo dad say to his kid when he left the herd?"

"Bye Son."

"What do you call two male cows who read Scripture?"

"Bi-bulls."

"What did the mother llama say to the baby llama pushing the doorbell?"

"'I'm Mama Llama Ding-Dong!'"

They were so bad we couldn't help laughing. It started raining, but we didn't care. We just kept pedaling, passing others who slowed.

I told Jeff about the verse in Proverbs I had read a few days earlier, and he said, "What did the kid with cancer say to the guy who rode 200 miles with him?"

"I give up."

"Thanks for being my friend."

CHAPTER 65

❀ Ashley ❀

I felt caught between two cases—three counting the middle school—and I wished Bryce would get back to help me sort them out. I took a break to clear my head and drove my ATV to the Morris farm to check on our alpaca, Amazing Grace. She was prancing around her mother when I arrived.

Mr. Morris had given Bryce and me the alpaca after an adventure while he and his family were out of town. Alpacas are gentle animals with really soft fur that people use for sweaters and other clothes. They have long necks and big eyes like camels, but they're a lot cuter.

I greeted Mr. Morris and gave Grace a treat.

Mom's phone buzzed. It was Bryce. "Ash," he said, "pray for Jeff. He just collapsed."

CHAPTER 66

☻ *Bryce* ☻

Jeff and I had stopped at a barn in a field not far from the road. We limped over to join the others watching the roiling clouds. Jeff's parents had just pulled up when I heard a commotion and turned to see Jeff on the ground.

As Jeff was being carried to the van, he waved and said he was okay, but I could tell everyone was scared.

The rain came harder as we settled in. Several in our group gathered in a corner, holding hands and praying.

A half hour later Mr. Alexander asked if Jeff had told me about his severe headaches all day.

"No," I said. "We were even joking most of the ride."

Mr. Alexander sat beside me. "He wants to finish more than anything, but I just don't see it."

"He wouldn't have to even pedal," I said. "All he has to do is hang on."

"Some of the other riders want to help. They can give you a rest—you switch and ride their bikes for a while."

I shook my head. "No way. I want to do this. If I get to where I can't go on, I'll ask for help. As long as Jeff gets to finish."

The rain pecked at the metal roof like chickens searching for food. A mist swept across the valley. The temperature dropped, and it almost felt cold enough to snow. Yes, even in June. Trust me— I've seen it.

"I'll bet this is hard for you and your wife," I said.

"We've been letting go of Jeff since the day he was born," Mr. Alexander said. "That's a parent's job. You watch him take his first step. You see him go to school. I was looking forward to teaching Jeff to drive. Sending him to college . . ."

His voice trailed off as he looked out at the plains. "This is every parent's nightmare. We've trusted God with Jeff since he was born. We need to trust him now even more."

CHAPTER 67

✖ Ashley ✖

Mom and I taped the afternoon news, which carried a story about the bike ride. They showed the beginning, which I hadn't seen before, including a tight shot of Jeff and a little of Bryce's backside, which I thought was funny. I couldn't wait to show him.

"Many have come to know this young man, Jeff Alexander, through his column in a local newspaper," the reporter said. "Some have even made per-mile donation pledges to fight cancer on his behalf. But today, Jeff is fighting to make his dream become a reality."

Leigh walked in and joined us to watch.

The report showed Jeff being helped from his parents' van and a group of riders staring at the rain. Looking exhausted, Jeff stood in a patch of light at the barn's edge. His face was pale as a ghost's.

"We've come a long way," Jeff said, "but we've got farther to go. I don't want to let anybody down. I just hope I can finish."

Mom wiped away a tear. Leigh just stared. It was strange watching a friend of mine on TV. The last shot showed Bryce and Jeff looking out at the rain. The news showed a phone number for people who wanted to contribute.

I wanted to ask Leigh what she thought, but I didn't want to get into another fight. Dylan came in with two eggbeaters, pretending he was holding a microphone and singing some song he had made up.

A picture flashed on the screen and I yelled, "Quiet!" Dylan's lip quivered and he ran out. I felt bad, but I couldn't help it. The picture was of Gunnar.

"New evidence tonight in the disappearance of a Red Rock man missing more than two weeks. Police say Gunnar Roberts was at a local grocery store the day before he went missing. An investigation of Roberts's vehicle, found submerged in a nearby lake, led authorities to a receipt from the store. A surveillance video clearly shows the man in the store.

"Red Rock police ask that you call the number on the screen if you have any information on his whereabouts."

CHAPTER 68

☺ *Bryce* ☺

The clouds finally broke, and the temperature warmed. We headed to the top of Wilkerson Pass, which is a whole lot easier to talk about than actually do. On several stretches I had to get off and push, and I admit there were times when I almost took the others up on their offers to trade places. Gary rode alongside, his leg muscles bulging as he pushed toward the summit, all the time urging me on and telling Jeff to just hang in there.

When we finally got to the welcome center, everybody clapped and raised their fists. My legs were as wobbly as an old chair. We were almost at 10,000 feet, and it felt like I had carried the bike the whole way. Jeff looked worn out too, but he still smiled. People crowded around him and took pictures.

"It's pretty much downhill from here, isn't it?" Jeff said.

Gary nodded. "We'll camp tonight at Lake George, about 2,000 feet below us. Colorado Springs is about 40 more miles from there."

It seemed as if we coasted into Lake George, a really small town with one motel, one store, and some areas for camping. I ate burgers from the grill. Jeff took his medicine and said he wasn't hungry.

When the sun went down, the stars shone brighter than anywhere else I'd ever seen them. Maybe it was getting through all those clouds that did it, but it looked like you could reach out and touch them.

We were in our sleeping bags, staring out the tent flap, when Jeff said, "Do you think angels can see us?"

"Another bad joke?"

"No, I mean it. Are there angels up there right now who can look at us?"

I shrugged. "Why would they? I can think of about a million better things to do."

"But there are guardian angels, right? Ones God sends to protect people?"

"I believe in those," I said, reminding him about Sam and Ashley and Dylan and me plunging into the lake in our car and almost not getting out alive. "I think angels were right there with us."

Jeff smiled. "Mine's named Todd."

"Excuse me?"

"That's what I call him. He doesn't talk to me or anything, but I know he's there."

"Well, tell Todd good night for me."

CHAPTER 69

✾ Ashley ✾

"Whatever happened to your uncle?" I asked Hayley as we headed to her aunt's house the next morning.

"My parents don't talk about it much, but I think he ran off when Gunnar was little. Nobody's heard from him in years."

That made me feel even more sorry for her aunt. At best, her son had abandoned her. At worst, he had been hurt or killed.

Hayley and I sat with her aunt in her living room. "The receipt they talked about on the news was from King Soopers," she said. "Gunnar bought a bunch of supplies like he was going away for a year."

"That's good," Hayley said. "It means he's probably still alive."

Her aunt shook her head. "Seems clear he was running from someone."

"Like those goons who came here the other day," I said.

She gave me a startled look. "You're never to talk about those men. Do you understand?"

"Why, Mrs. Roberts?" I said. "They might be the key to where Gunnar is."

"I told you what they threatened, and I don't want to say it again."

CHAPTER 70

☺ *Bryce* ☺

I woke to birds chirping. A mist rose from Lake George, which is a funny name for a lake. I could see it as a name for a grandfather but not a lake. I wondered why they didn't name it Lake Bob or Lake Walt.

Jeff awoke like an 80-year-old man, stiff and grunting. He threw back the sleeping bag, and I noticed his pale arms and legs. "Last day," he said.

"How does it feel? You're actually going to finish this thing."

He groaned as he put on his socks. "I've dreamed of this for months. Now, part of me doesn't want it to end."

I nodded. It made me sad to think of the bike ride ending too.

People gathered around the campfire outside, cooking breakfast, drinking coffee, and talking softly.

"How's he doing?" Gary said.

"Ready to finish, and not ready at the same time."

Gary smiled. "We've got a surprise for him at the end. There are a couple more challenging hills, so I can help if you want, but you're going to bring him home."

We weren't that far from the Florissant Fossil Beds, and I wished we could spend a couple of days there. There were so many things we could have done, but we had to keep moving.

With some hard riding we reached Woodland Park by late morning. If we went over the mountain behind the town, we would be at the Air Force Academy, and a few miles beyond that lay Red Rock.

The local police blocked traffic as we rode through Woodland Park, which has a lot of shops and restaurants. Some people looked ticked that we were tying up the road, but others stood clapping. Some waved American flags.

After lunch and a little rest, we headed down the winding road to Colorado Springs. Pikes Peak stood like a brown soldier to our right. Funny how it looks different from different angles. From our house, Pikes Peak looks long and wide, like you could easily walk up it. From this angle it looked steep and impossible to climb. I've heard that the first white people who saw it thought you might die if you tried to get to the top.

We wound down to Manitou Springs, which also has a lot of artsy shops. The Cog Railway there takes you to the top of Pikes Peak. When we passed the Cave of the Winds, I remembered the first time I had met Jeff. It was on a trip to the Cliff Dwellings, where ancient people had carved their homes right into the rock.

Jeff had introduced himself to me while I bought an arrowhead necklace in the gift shop. He said he was sorry to hear that my dad had been killed. It had been a few years since it had happened, but it felt good that he said something.

"We could turn right and go straight up Pikes Peak," Jeff said, and I turned to see him smiling weakly.

"Maybe next year," I said.

Gary held up a hand in front of us, signaling a turn. We turned left into the entrance to the Garden of the Gods, and the whole group headed for the visitors' center. Police blocked roads, and cars honked at us. People waved like they knew who we were.

We stopped in front of one of the huge red rock formations, and everybody got off their bikes. By this time, friends and family members had caught up and wanted to take pictures. Some were crying. I guess remembering loved ones who had died from cancer. Jeff's parents took photos and shot video.

Gary came up to me and said, "We still have a little farther to go. You okay?"

I nodded. I wanted to get back on the bike and help Jeff finish. And I had a good idea of my own to make the end of the trip even more memorable.

CHAPTER 71

✺ Ashley ✺

Sam came home early from the airport and got us all together
for the trip to the Springs. I think it was hard for Mom to have Bryce
gone this long without being able to do more than talk on the phone.
Dylan had colored Bryce three pictures—though you really couldn't
tell what they were besides crayon circles with eyes and smiling
mouths.

Leigh acted like she didn't care if she went or stayed, but I sus-
pected she was getting more interested in Jeff's story and wanted to
see how things turned out.

The trip was originally scheduled to end at the Garden of the

Gods, but an e-mail to the families said it would now end at the Olympic training center in downtown Colorado Springs.

We got there about an hour before the bicyclists were to arrive, and the parking lot was already nearly full. We took our place on Boulder Street and sat on a blanket. It was hard to keep Dylan in one place, so I took him a couple of blocks away to a park.

I pushed him on the swing set, trying to let him go as high as he wanted. As I kept a close eye on him and urged him to hang on tight, he yelled, "Higher!"

But then I heard yelling and clapping from the crowd. "Time to go see Bryce," I said.

CHAPTER 72

☺ *Bryce* ☺

We rode out of the Garden of the Gods toward the city. Police blocked traffic, and soon we neared the statue of General Palmer, the man who founded Colorado Springs. Jeff was pedaling now too.

"We're going to make it," he said, panting. "We're really going to make it."

"Two hundred miles," I said.

"I couldn't have done it without you."

When we reached Boulder Street, I signaled to Gary and everyone pulled to the side. I hopped off and turned to Jeff.

He looked like he had lost his mother at an amusement park. "What?"

"You're taking us home," I said. "Get in the front."

His mouth dropped and he just sat there.

"Alexander!" Gary shouted. "You're holding us up."

"Yeah, get a move on, Jeff!" someone else said. Others joined in, and Jeff smiled as wide as I'd ever seen him. We traded places.

Everyone else stayed back as Jeff pulled ahead. Then they fell in behind us. I didn't have to worry about steering, so I looked back at hundreds of riders who had become my friends over the last four days. We had started as separate riders, and now we had one goal—seeing Jeff finish.

Police-car lights flashed as they followed our convoy. We headed up Boulder Street, pedaling past people, cars, and more flashing lights. We were getting close.

Jeff stood to pedal and dipped his head. I could tell he was crying.

"You okay?" I said.

"I just wish this wouldn't end," he said.

"Hey, I told you, we'll do it again next year."

Jeff nodded, but we both knew. There would be no next year.

"Something I want to tell you," Jeff said as we passed cheering throngs.

"I'm all ears," I said.

"DM will be looking for one last box. You can show it to them."

"Who's DM?" I shouted.

"Just listen. We've been there together only once, but that's where you'll find the clue. Go there and you'll solve the mystery."

"I have no idea what you're talking about!"

"I recorded some thoughts on my machine for the last column. Think you could help?"

"People don't want to hear from me, Jeff. They want to hear from you."

"I'm tired. I'd feel better knowing you could handle this."

"Fine, but I'll need to get Ashley involved. She's a lot better writer than—"

"No, I want you to do it. Promise me you'll do it yourself."

"Okay, but the people at the paper will have to work overtime to correct my spelling."

Jeff chuckled, then turned to face a sea of people. The other riders came up behind us and made a long line across the road. We heard the *click*ing and *clack*ing of their bikes and the roar of the crowd.

CHAPTER 73

✖ Ashley ✖

Dylan and I made it back as the bicycles came into view. Jeff's parents were at the front of the crowd, holding each other and crying. More people had gathered on either side of the road, and a lot of them had on the same colorful uniforms. Then it hit me—they were real Olympic athletes.

One of the gold medalists in swimming raced to the other side of the street. He joined the gold medalist in cycling. They strung a paper tape across the street, the kind runners break when they come in first place.

"Where's Bryce?" Dylan said.

"He's coming," I said.

I put Dylan on my shoulders and tried to find a spot where we could see everyone. There was no chanting, no music, no one singing, just steady clapping, whistling, and shouts.

The news truck with its big satellite dish on top stood at the side of the street, and a cameraman pushed through the crowd.

"Bryce!" Dylan shouted.

Jeff was in front, Bryce right behind him, smiling from ear to ear, his fist in the air.

I found Mom crying, waving, and yelling. Sam's mustache wrinkled as he smiled and clapped. His whistle was so loud I could tell it a mile away.

Most surprising was Leigh. She was yelling, "Yay, Bryce! Go, Jeff!" and giving them a thumbs-up, as into it as any of us.

When Jeff and Bryce broke the tape and passed the finish line, the crowd surrounded them, and a man hoisted Jeff on his shoulders and paraded him around. Someone hung a gold medal around Jeff's neck, and it looked real.

I couldn't imagine a happier moment for Jeff.

And then something happened.

Commotion.

People yelling.

"Get back! Get back!"

I swung Dylan down and held his hand.

There was a siren. An ambulance. They loaded someone inside.

Jeff.

CHAPTER 74

☺ *Bryce* ☺

Everything seemed fine until Jeff crossed the finish line. I could hear him in my helmet—laughing with the Olympic athletes and getting picked up by Gary.

Then he grabbed his head, slumped, and groaned. I yelled, but I could tell no one heard me. Jeff fell when Gary set him down. A TV cameraman crowded in, but I pushed him away. I know the guy was just doing his job, but Jeff needed help. Anyway, I wanted people to see him finishing, not falling.

Jeff still had his helmet on when they loaded him into the ambulance. Just before they closed the door, he raised his hand and tried to sit up. "Bryce," he said, his voice weak.

"Right here," I said into my microphone.

"Don't forget to—"

The door shut, and all I could hear through his mike were emergency medical technicians removing his helmet, talking to him, and giving him oxygen.

I found my family, and we rushed to the hospital. Gary and others from the trip showed up in the waiting room. The TV reporter came in and the cameraman. He had long hair and a face like the guys you see on romance book covers.

"Sorry about pushing you," I said.

He put a hand on my shoulder. "I understand. How's your friend?"

"Don't know yet. Did you get a shot of us at the finish line?"

He smiled. "We were live at five. The sun was streaming down on you guys through the trees—almost like God was smiling at you—and I had a great angle. Probably the best live shot I've ever got—except for how things turned out."

Everybody looked up as Mr. Alexander came out of the emergency room. "Doctor says it was probably just the excitement," he said. "At least that's what he hopes. Jeff passed out on the way here, woke up once, but he's sleeping now. They're going to move him to intensive care. That's all we know. We do want to say how much we appreciate all you've done. . . ." Then he broke down, and several moved to comfort him.

A nurse approached. "Are you Bryce? Mrs. Alexander asked if you'd like to come back."

I followed her. The place smelled funny, like everything was too clean. I felt grungy in my riding clothes and carrying my helmet.

The nurse pulled back a curtain revealing Jeff sleeping, a tube hooked to his arm. It looked painful, but Jeff has been through this before.

"He asked for you," Mrs. Alexander said. "Wanted to know what happened to the bike."

"Just like him," I said. "I hadn't even thought about it."

CHAPTER 75

Ashley

We left the hospital when Jeff was moved to the intensive care unit, still asleep.

"I can't believe you rode that whole way, Bryce," Leigh said.

"I can't believe Jeff did," I said.

At dinner Bryce ate like a starving man. Then we went to his room. He told me what Jeff had said at the end of the ride.

"Another box?" I said. "Who's looking for it?"

"Someone he called DM."

"That's the same thing the guy on the phone said. 'Tim Minaro with DM.'"

Bryce shook his head. I told him what I had learned about Gunnar. Bryce wrote Gunnar clues on white cards and memorabilia clues on blue ones. "I don't see any connection," he said.

"But this construction guy, Jeppeson, might have been at the Alexanders' house. I saw a box in his truck."

Bryce scratched his head. "Could Gunnar be involved? If he's short of money, it could make sense."

"How would he have gotten into the house? Everything points to somebody inside."

"But it doesn't seem to be the housekeeper or anybody else we've considered," he said.

"What about Jeff's mom and dad? Is there any reason they would ask for your help if they were the ones—?"

Bryce shook his head. "Nah. This is like one of those word jumbles you do. We have a lot of the letters, but none of them fit."

I moved the cards around. The whole thing looked like a jigsaw puzzle with all the pieces the same.

Someone knocked on the door. "News is coming on," Leigh said.

CHAPTER 76

☺ *Bryce* ☺

I wanted to watch, but I was afraid it might be bad news about Jeff. The report began live outside the Olympic training center.

The female reporter stood alone, the Olympic circles behind her and flags flying. "Earlier today this street teemed with people congratulating a brave young man and many others who rode their bikes for cancer research. But the finish of the 200-mile ride turned quickly from a dream to a nightmare."

The footage showed us in Vail. It felt like 10 years since we had been there. Our route was charted on a map. Then they flashed a picture of Jeff's column. A spokesman from the cancer research group said they had received a record number of contributions since the trip started.

"It wasn't a race, but the young man who dreamed about this grueling bike hike finished first, with the help of a friend."

Ashley punched me on the shoulder as the video switched to Jeff and me crossing the finish line. The cameraman was right. The sunshine through the clouds and trees cast a golden glow on the scene.

The crowd engulfed us, and Jeff rose on Gary's shoulders.

"There," I said. "Right there. Jeff grunts and goes down."

They showed the hospital, then Jeff's mom and dad outside, arm in arm. Mrs. Alexander tearfully thanked everyone who had given money.

One of the Olympic athletes said, "A lot of people think we're heroes, but that kid has more courage and determination than anyone."

"There's still no word on Jeff's condition," the reporter concluded. "But his parents and friends ask for your prayers."

Our phone began ringing, and people asked if we had seen the news. Then another call came, and Sam asked Mom to join him in the kitchen.

CHAPTER 77

❦ Ashley ❦

I helped Bryce get Dylan ready for bed. Dylan put his arms around Bryce's neck. "I missed you," he said, before sticking his thumb in his mouth.

We headed downstairs, but I stopped when I saw Mom and Sam waiting at the bottom.

"No," I said.

We followed them into the living room, and they turned off the TV.

Leigh said, "Hey, I was watching that!" But she fell silent when she saw Mom's and Sam's faces.

"That was Jeff's dad," Mom said.

"Is he gone?" Bryce whispered.

Mom looked at the floor. "No. But his immune system is low. It doesn't look good." She put a hand over her mouth.

Sam took over, his growly voice even lower than usual. "The doctor couldn't believe he'd made it the whole way. Said he had to have somebody really strong helping him."

"It wasn't me," Bryce said. Then he whispered, "Todd." Or maybe "God." I'd have to ask him about that.

"I'm sorry," Sam continued, "but you need to be prepared for the worst."

"It's not fair," Leigh said. "That kid never did anything to anybody. Why can't God do something for him?" She looked down, and her hair covered her face.

Bryce seemed in shock.

All I could do was pray silently for the doctors, the Alexanders, and Jeff. Then I thanked him that Jeff had Bryce, a friend who stuck close to him through all those miles. It struck me that I rarely prayed about Bryce.

In the Bible it says something about the prayer of a righteous person having great power and producing wonderful results. I didn't feel much like a righteous person, and to be honest, I wasn't asking for a miracle. I just wanted us to somehow get through this awful thing.

CHAPTER 78

☺ *Bryce* ☺

I dropped into bed and fell asleep fast. When I woke up I felt like I had been run over by a cement truck. I trudged downstairs and asked Mom if we could visit Jeff.

"He's a little better this morning, Bryce. He might even get to come home soon."

"Can I call him?"

"No, not yet. Let's just see what the day holds."

That made me want to find his missing stuff all the more, and I told Ashley we were going to do it before Jeff came back.

"Let's go to the school and see if we can find that Jeppeson guy," she said.

I still didn't see the connection, but Jeff had said we should give DM the last box—that I could show it to them. And that we'd been there once together.

"If we find out what DM stands for," she said, "we'll solve this thing."

The middle school still had a big tarp covering something. Ashley pointed. "That's Jeppeson's truck."

We were heading across the parking lot toward it when my cell phone rang. It was Mom, and she seemed to be fighting to keep from crying. "I need you to come home," she said.

"Why?" I said. "What's wrong?"

Sam's voice came on. "Bryce, just come home."

CHAPTER 79

❀ Ashley ❀

It was a long ride. Bryce rode ahead of me, zigzagging on his ATV through the field near our house. I tried to think of anything it could be other than Jeff.

Minutes later we were in the living room. Mom and Sam sat next to each other on the couch. Sam rubbed his arms, not looking at either of us. Mom stared through cloudy eyes.

Bryce tossed his helmet on a chair.

"Sit," Mom said, patting the couch.

I sat next to her, and she wrapped her arms around me.

Bryce just stood there looking like he wanted to run, to be anywhere but here. "Tell us," he said.

Sam cleared his throat and looked at the floor. "The Alexanders thought Jeff was coming out of it, but he's taken a turn."

Bryce screwed up his face. "Just tell me!"

Mom sat forward. "They don't think it will be much longer, hon."

Leigh appeared at the top of the stairs with Dylan, tears in her eyes.

I buried my face in Mom's arms.

"I want to go see him," Bryce said.

CHAPTER 80

☺ *Bryce* ☺

My legs felt as rubbery walking into the hospital as they had at the end of the bike trip. The alcohol smells, the shiny hallways, families gathered in the waiting room, all of it got to me.

The nurses in the cancer ICU really looked stressed. It must be hard taking care of dying people, especially getting attached to kids and then seeing them only get worse, no matter how hard you work.

"He's hanging on," Mr. Alexander said. "They did a brain scan and found a big change since last week. The tumor is pressing against some vital areas."

"Can they do another operation?" I said.

Mr. Alexander frowned. "I wish. The way it's positioned, they really can't."

He said more stuff that I didn't understand. I just wanted to see my friend. Finally he walked me to Jeff's room. Mrs. Alexander forced a smile and took my hand.

Jeff's cheeks were sunken, and there were tubes hooked to him and machines beeping and blipping.

I just stared, feeling helpless. This was way harder than I expected.

"I think he needs our permission," Mrs. Alexander whispered.

"Our permission?"

She spoke so softly I was sure nobody else could hear. "The doctors say something happens near the end. The patient cares so much about those he's leaving that it's hard for him to let go."

"You mean, we have to let him know it's okay to . . . ?"

Mrs. Alexander nodded. "We've told him. Maybe he needs to hear it from you." She stepped back.

I pulled a chair next to the bed and leaned toward Jeff. For the past few days I had heard Jeff's breathing through the microphone in our helmets. I had no idea what he had been going through and what the headaches really meant.

"Hey, buddy," I said softly. "That was some finish."

His eyelids flickered and his hand twitched.

"You should have seen us on TV. You would have thought we'd won a gold medal."

I told Jeff how much money had been raised, and I imagined I saw him smile. I was supposed to be letting him go, but part of me didn't want to. I wanted to go to the eighth grade with Jeff.

But it wasn't fair to make him hang on like this. He was headed to a lot better place, where no tumors grow and people don't die in plane crashes.

"Remember what you said about seeing my dad?" I whispered. We had talked about it one night during the trip. Jeff said he wanted to find my dad and talk with him once he got to heaven. "Don't forget to tell him I love him and miss him. Tell him about the bike ride and how we worked together. Tell him my mom's a Christian now—that'll make him really happy. And tell him Ashley and I are Christians too and that we'll all be together one day."

I paused, but I didn't sense any response. "You can go now, Jeff. Your mom and dad know how much you love them, and the rest of us do too." A tear rolled down his cheek, and I'm sure he was trying to smile. "And don't forget to thank Todd for me."

CHAPTER 81

✖ Ashley ✖

When Bryce got home he looked like someone had sucked the marrow from his bones. He didn't want to talk.

We heard nothing from the hospital the rest of the night, and I had a hard time sleeping. I wondered if we'd ever get Jeff's things back, but now a few signed footballs and baseballs didn't seem to matter.

I dreamed that Hayley's cousin broke into our house and took Mom's computer—the one that has her book manuscripts on it. I ran after him and found myself in the hallway of the middle school. In my nightgown. Skeeter Messler offered his coat, but I ran into the gym. Everybody laughed at me, pointing and taking pictures.

The next few days went by slowly. Bryce slept a lot, trying to recuperate from the trip. We got an update from Jeff's parents each day, but we hated bothering them.

On Sunday, Mom drove Bryce, Dylan, and me to church (Sam and Leigh only go on Christmas and Easter), and it felt good to be with my friends in Sunday school.

Our youth pastor had Bryce tell about his trip, and we all prayed for Jeff. Some kids acted out a couple of dramas that were pretty funny, but I couldn't laugh.

Our church service usually begins with some kind of praise song, but when the musicians ended the prelude, our senior pastor, Reverend Jackson, walked to the pulpit. "The Lord gives and the Lord takes away," he said. "Blessed be the name of the Lord."

A hush fell over the congregation.

"As most of you know, we've had the privilege of knowing a special young man in this church the past few years."

Jeff's seventh-grade photo flashed on the screen, showing him smiling big, like he couldn't stop laughing.

"Today, our loss is heaven's gain. Jeff Alexander went to be with Jesus just minutes ago. His parents knew you would want to know." Pastor Jackson looked down at his Bible.

I saw kids crying. Bryce sat staring out the window that faces the mountains.

"I wish I had the answers to the questions running through all our minds right now," Pastor Jackson said with a shaky voice. "All I know is that when one of his dear friends passed away, Jesus wept. He feels the heartache, but he also holds our friend in his arms. And someday we'll see Jeff again because of Jesus."

CHAPTER 82

☾ *Bryce* ☾

Cars ringed the Alexanders' house. An older woman an-
swered the door, and I guessed she was Jeff's grandmother. She was
red-eyed, like everybody else. Jeff's mom saw Ashley and me and
rushed to hug us.

"I came for the digital recorder," I said. "Jeff made some notes on
it and asked me to write his last newspaper column."

She nodded. "We put his things in his room. You can go on up."

Jeff's helmet lay on the bed along with his dress clothes. His parents
had probably picked them out for his funeral. I felt guilty being in
there, like we were on holy ground.

The recorder was on his nightstand. As we turned to leave I noticed a poster on Jeff's wall. The painting was from a runner's perspective, and golden sunlight filtered down to red rocks. The next step was a drop, a precipice over a huge chasm. It was clear the runner was going to jump to the other side to a beautiful forest and waterfall.

Underneath the scene were these words: *Success is the ability to focus not on what's behind or around, but on what's ahead.*

CHAPTER 83

Ashley

Bryce took the laptop computer to his room. I offered to help him write the column, but he wanted to do it himself. He asked if I'd phone the editor at the paper and tell her it was coming.

When I told her what Bryce was doing, she said, "I'm so sorry about Jeff. I can't imagine how hard it must be for his parents."

She told me she would run Bryce's article in the morning with the story on Jeff's death, "if he can transmit it to me tonight."

I waited in my room, tried listening to music, lighting a candle, and writing in my journal, but I couldn't get my mind off Jeff. Mom gave me a book about heaven that had lots of quotes from the Bible and famous Christians.

I found one from a man named C. S. Lewis who wrote a lot of books about being a Christian. "I must keep alive in myself the desire for my true country, which I shall not find till after death; I must never let it get snowed under or turned aside; I must make it the main object of life to press on to that other country and to help others do the same."

CHAPTER 84

☻ *Bryce* ☻

It was weird hearing Jeff's voice on the recorder. Most were random thoughts. The color of the trees. The way the mountains looked as we rode past. Jeff had a great eye, and he noticed things I didn't.

I typed everything he said. How was I going to make a column out of this? Why had he wanted me to write it myself? Ashley would have been a big help. My mom could have done it in her sleep. I started three times, then erased what I'd written.

Mom says she sometimes starts in the middle of what she wants to say, then goes back and writes the beginning. I tried that and found the words coming easier. I tried to write what Jeff would say.

Mom called us to dinner, but I kept working. I knew she'd understand. When I finished, I went back and wrote a beginning. It was okay, but I tinkered with it for a long time. Finally I saved and printed it.

"Want me to take a look?" Mom said. She put a pencil behind her ear and walked around the dining-room table, reading. I kept waiting for her to mark it up like my English teacher, but finally she stopped in front of our big windows, turned, and gently set the paper on the table.

"I wouldn't change a thing," she said, tears in her eyes.

CHAPTER 85

JEFF'S DIARY

by Bryce Timberline
I've known Jeff Alexander since I moved to Red Rock a few years ago. I was excited when he asked me to join him on a long bike trip to raise money for cancer research, and I want to thank everyone who gave money to support Jeff and the cause. To be honest, I didn't know if we'd be able to finish.

If you've read his columns, you know how much Jeff loved life. As we rode, he kept noticing things I didn't. Like the boulders he called "dinosaur eggs." And the way Pikes Peak changes with the way the sun hits it. It's the same mountain all day, but it looks different at different times.

When we were just about finished, Jeff moved to the front seat of our bike. He wasn't well, but this was his dream, and he pushed himself to the end.

Jeff wasn't perfect. He was a teenager, which meant he got angry, was selfish, said things he regretted, and even forgot to do his homework a few times. He was not a saint, but he did have the biggest heart of anybody I've ever known. I wish there were some way to prove that, but you'll just have to take my word.

It's hard saying good-bye to someone who has meant so much to so many people. If Jeff were writing this instead of me, he'd want to tell you how much God loves you and wants you to know him. He'd probably describe the last sunset he saw behind Pikes Peak. But the last thing Jeff would want you to be would be sorry for him.

The truth is, this morning when Jeff took his last breath, he got to see the most beautiful sight ever. That any of us will ever see. He got to be with the one who loved him so much that he died for him. Jeff doesn't have to worry about tumors anymore, and he doesn't have to deal with headaches and blood work and hospital rooms.

If you think of Jeff in the weeks to come, I hope you'll pray for his mom and dad and those of us who knew him. If you're like me, you have questions about why it happened to him and how God could allow it. I learned at church this week that it's okay to ask those questions, but be open to letting God speak to you through the Bible.

I promised Jeff I would write this for him. Thanks for reading it.

CHAPTER 86

✖ Ashley ✖

I felt numb the whole next day. The same feelings came back as after we learned our dad had died in the plane crash. We wanted the whole world to stop, but it didn't. Everything kept on going like it was normal. Bryce and I didn't feel like doing anything, but we agreed it would be good to keep going with our investigation.

"Okay, back to the last stuff Jeff said. What's it mean?"

Bryce scratched his head. "I've been trying to think of some place we went only once. The whole bike trip was the first time we'd been to those places. But I still don't know who DM is. And how could he know we were trying to solve a mystery?"

"Maybe he figured it out."

"Yeah, I still had my helmet on when I talked with you."

Ashley snapped her fingers. "Wait, maybe he meant the trip you, me, and Hayley took."

Bryce stared at me.

At the same time we both said, "The tree house!"

We wanted to take our ATVs, but Sam has a rule about us not riding on main roads. Bryce suggested we call Hayley, and we met her at her aunt's house. From there it was up the hill toward the haunted house.

We brought Hayley up to date on what we had learned, and she said they had heard nothing further about Gunnar. We rode side by side until a car came. Then we rode single file. Once a dark car passed us and kicked up so much dust we had to pull over and let it settle.

I couldn't help thinking of Jeff. It seemed like only a few days ago that we were riding and laughing together. The road seemed even longer now. Finally, the house came into view. Instead of stopping and enjoying it, the three of us raced around the hill, past the house, and on to the graveyard. The way the shadows hit it made it look spooky.

I looked for the spot where Jeff had said his grave would be. There was no gravedigger in sight or upturned dirt.

We climbed up the tree and looked around. There were some old magazines piled in a corner and a couple of stumps Jeff used for seats. Jeff kept a waterproof radio on a branch, but we couldn't find it. Bryce said Jeff and his dad had built it together and kept it up here to listen to Rockies games.

There was some plastic in the corner, and Bryce reached it before me. He pulled it away, but the space underneath was empty.

"I guess this tarp is in case it rains."

Hayley sat on one of the stumps. We tried to think of any place all three of us had been with Jeff in the past few weeks. "I can't think of anywhere else unless it's in there," Hayley said, pointing to the haunted house.

Bryce looked at the house. "It's worth a try."

CHAPTER 87

☺ *Bryce* ☺

The sun was going down behind the mountain when we walked inside the run-down kitchen. The old house was so big, I didn't know where to start. Ashley walked quickly into the dining room, and I followed. On top of a ramshackle table sat a box, its top covered.

"This wasn't here the last time we came," Ashley said.

I grabbed the cover and pulled it off. We all gasped. The signed football, several pictures, and other memorabilia were inside.

"How did Jeff leave this here without us seeing?" Hayley said. "He stayed behind while we came in, didn't he?"

I nodded. "He came in the secret entrance, but I don't think he would have had time to put it here."

Ashley shook her head. "I don't get it."

"Maybe Jeff didn't bring this stuff in here," Hayley said. "Maybe it was somebody else."

"Who?"

"The construction guy," Ashley said.

"How would Jeff know about that guy?" I said.

"Wait, is this all the stuff?" Hayley said.

"No," I said. "There's a lot still missing."

A board creaked above us, and the three of us held our breath. I knew the windows upstairs were broken and that wind blew through and made noise, but this didn't sound like wind.

"Keep talking like we didn't hear anything," I whispered.

"What are you going to do?" Ashley said.

I didn't answer and stole outside through the kitchen. Ashley said something, and as I passed the broken window at the side I heard Hayley give a nervous laugh.

I found the secret entrance and slipped inside, taking the stairs two at a time, slowly, testing them to make sure I didn't make noise. I held on to the sides of the narrow passage, supporting myself by pushing my hands against both sides. At the top of the stairs I paused and listened. All I could hear was Ashley and Hayley talking below.

I sucked in some air, grabbed the doorknob, and burst into the room.

A man with a full beard jumped back, losing his footing and tumbling. It was like a tiger being scared by a kitten.

Something on the floor caught my eye. I walked forward, my stomach in a knot. "That's Jeff's radio. What are you doing with it?"

He looked at it, then scrambled to his feet and headed for the door. He stopped short, staring at the hallway like another kitten had jumped at him.

Hayley and Ashley reached the top of the stairs.

"Gunnar?" Hayley said. "Is that you?"

CHAPTER 88

✖ Ashley ✖

Gunnar reeled when he saw Hayley. She stepped toward him like she wanted to hug him, but he moved back, looking at Bryce and the passage he was blocking.

"We've all been worried about you," Hayley said. "Have you been here all this time?"

Gunnar clenched his teeth. "You don't know what you've just done. All three of you. You have to promise you won't tell anybody where I am."

"Why?" Bryce said. "Give us a reason."

"Yeah, especially since you stole a sick kid's stuff," I said.

"What are you talking about?"

I pointed at the floor. "The radio and the stuff downstairs. It's Jeff's. Why'd you steal it?"

"You're crazy," he said.

My stomach boiled. "Jeff's dead. What were you going to do, sell it after you waited long enough?"

"I found a box under the plastic out there and brought it in. The radio too." He ran his hands through his brown hair. I'd seen Gunnar's picture at Hayley's aunt's house and in the newspaper. Though he looked haggard, there was something about him that was kind of cute.

"You have to leave and not tell anybody you saw me," he said.

"We're not going anywhere until you tell us what's going on," Bryce said. I could tell he meant it by the tone of his voice. "Why did you drown your Jeep? Why'd you leave your dog?"

"How is Jenny?"

"Fine," Hayley said. "But answer the question. What's going on?"

Gunnar paced in front of the window. Cobwebs hung from the ceiling and wafted in the breeze. This was the man everyone in Colorado was looking for.

Bryce pulled out his cell phone. "I've had enough of this."

"Okay, okay, I'll tell you. Put that away."

Bryce shoved the phone in his pocket and crossed his arms, still standing in front of the exit.

"I got in some trouble," Gunnar said. "I had to run."

Bryce waved a hand and pulled his phone out again. "Forget it. I'm calling the—"

"All right, I borrowed some money from some goons and couldn't pay them back. I had to make it look like I was hurt or something."

"Those guys who came to your house?" Hayley said.

Gunnar's face turned white. "What did they look like?"

"Gorillas," I said. "Nicely dressed gorillas. Arms the size of tree trunks. Sunglasses. Shiny car. One of them looked like a shark with his shiny suit."

"That's them," he said, rubbing the back of his neck. "I didn't think they'd bother Mom." He turned. "That kid who was with you—did he really die?"

Bryce nodded. "Yesterday."

"You gotta believe me. I didn't take his stuff. I was just looking through it and found the radio. There was a videodisc in there too. Had the name *Bryce* on it."

"That's me," Bryce said.

"I'll get it for you." He rummaged through some plastic bags that looked like they were half trash, half uneaten stuff. "I know it's in here somewhere."

"Why did you need the money?" Hayley said.

He stopped rummaging and looked at her. "I made a few trips up to Cripple Creek."

"Gambling?" Bryce said.

Gunnar nodded. "I'd been up there a few times and had done pretty well. I thought if I could get out of the hole I was in and show Taryn, she'd change her mind about me."

"And you'd just quit gambling?"

"Yeah. That was the plan. But the more I played, the further behind I got. There was this guy offering loans. I didn't have much other than my Jeep, but it was enough to get a few thousand. And the few thousand turned into more."

"Why don't you just go back and explain—?" Hayley said.

"There's no way I'm telling Mom," he said, cutting her off. "You know what my dad did to the family. I'd rather die."

CHAPTER 89

☻ *Bryce* ☻

This guy was a perfect illustration of about a hundred sermons I'd heard. The Prodigal Son (without the returning part), building your house on sand, sin catching up with you—all those verses were crouching on the floor of this abandoned house.

I've always heard it's best not to hide from your problems. That if you own up to your mistakes and face them, it's a lot better in the long run than trying to erase them by running. I didn't think Gunnar would take that advice, but I tried anyway.

"What if you went to those guys and said you'd pay them back? You could work out a deal where—"

"These guys don't make deals. You get a week—maybe two at

the most—and if you don't pay them, they break your arm. Add a week to that and you start seeing blood."

"It's been four weeks since you disappeared," Hayley said.

Gunnar nodded. "These guys aren't looking for me to send a get-well card. They want to make sure I never come back."

"Our church can help you," Ashley said. "They have meetings for people who have gambling problems."

"I can quit anytime I want," he said. "I just need some money."

I'd always heard the first step in getting out of trouble was realizing you had a problem. It didn't look like Gunnar was even ready to take a baby step in that direction.

Something rumbled outside, and Hayley stepped to the window. "Somebody's here."

"It's that dark car we saw at your aunt's house," Ashley said. "They're headed for the cemetery."

Gunnar raced to the window and ducked when he saw the car. His whole body shook. He grabbed a plastic bag with some supplies from the corner—his emergency stash, I guess—and turned to head downstairs.

"Where are you going?" I said.

"I have to get out of here. Can you stall those guys?"

"Come back with us," Hayley said.

"I'll be back. Tell my mom I love her and not to worry."

The car pulled up at the front, and doors slammed. I didn't want Gunnar to run, but if these guys caught him we'd probably never see him again. "Go out the secret exit. We'll cover you."

"Thanks." He slipped into the entrance.

I made sure the door was closed tightly.

We watched the goons with the big arms walk to the front porch. I took an unopened can of corn and knocked out the rest of a pane of glass. It crashed down on the outside roof, and the goons rushed into the house.

"What are we going to do?" Ashley said.

I held up a hand. "Just stay cool."

The three guys ran up the stairs. One held a gun in front of him, and I realized why Ashley had described him as looking like a shark. Ashley and Hayley stepped back as the three walked in and looked at the stash of bags and food scattered around the room.

The Shark put his gun back in its holster. "Followed you guys from Gunnar's house. You havin' a campout?" He spoke the way people on those New York cop shows do. Sounded like he was swallowing his words.

"Just came to find our friend's stuff," I said.

The Shark held his arms away from his sides as he walked around the room. I guess his muscles were so big he couldn't hold them closer.

The second one with long sideburns and a dark coat stepped forward. He spoke with a raspy voice and pointed at Hayley and Ashley. "We saw you two over at Gunnar's house, didn't we?"

"She's his cousin," I said. "You know where Gunnar is?"

The man scowled.

The Shark rifled through the plastic bags. "Looks like somebody's been here awhile. This your stuff?"

I looked at Ashley and Hayley and motioned toward the hall. "Come on, let's go."

The third guy put a hand out. "Answer the question."

There's a feature on my phone that makes it ring. I stuck my hand in my pocket and pushed the button. It chirped on cue, and I opened it. "Yeah, Dad, we're at the haunted house." I looked at the guy with the sideburns. "Okay, we're on our way."

"You're not going anywhere," The Shark said. He looked at the other two. "Search it."

When the guys moved into the hall, I saw our chance. I slammed the door, locked it, and raced for the secret passage.

"You kids have a nice time in there," The Shark said. "We can wait."

We were out the door and racing for our bikes. I prayed the guys wouldn't see us, but one yelled as we rode past the house. I was ahead of Ashley and Hayley, looking for any path or hiding place off the road.

The goons' car revved behind us.

We rounded a corner, and I spotted a small trail beside the road. The three of us got off just as the black car passed.

CHAPTER 90

✖ Ashley ✖

After the goons returned to search the house, Bryce called the police and we made our way to Hayley's aunt's house. When we told her we had seen Gunnar, she nearly fainted. The police officer said he'd check out the house and retrieve Jeff's things.

"What will you do to those goons?" I asked the officer.

"They're probably long gone by now," he said.

We went to the Alexanders' house on our way home and told them we'd found some of Jeff's things, but not all of them. They both seemed glad but were just as puzzled as we were about why Jeff would hide the stuff there.

I asked them about the construction guy, Clarke Jeppeson. Mr. Alexander said he'd never heard of him.

"Any idea what the initials DM stand for?" I said.

He shook his head.

"Maybe if we look a little further through Jeff's room," I said.

"You're more than welcome," the man said.

We looked through Jeff's closet and school backpack but didn't find any clues.

Finally Bryce sat on the bed. "Doesn't make sense that Jeff took the stuff himself. He would have known how much it would have hurt his mom and dad."

Mr. and Mrs. Alexander joined us in the room. I could tell it was hard for them to be here. You can prepare yourself for something for a long time and still not be ready for it.

"I knew you would come through for us," Mr. Alexander said. "Where do you think the rest of the stuff is?"

"We're hoping to find it soon," Bryce said.

"We can't thank you two enough for . . . well, for just being here," Mrs. Alexander said. "We'd like you to help us go through Jeff's things when we're ready . . . so we can donate them." Her lip quivered. "He asked us to give his clothes to someone who needed them as soon as we could manage. He said you two might help."

"We'd be glad to," Bryce said.

I couldn't imagine going through your son's stuff to give it away. Something didn't seem fair about it. I'd heard about grown-ups having to go through their parents' things to give away after they had died, but to give your teenage son's stuff away . . .

They offered us dinner and we stayed. The whole house was full of food, but none of us felt like eating. Mr. Alexander looked at his wife after we sat down and said we should pray. They were both so drained, I knew they wouldn't make it through.

I kicked Bryce under the table, and he started. "God, you know how much it hurts to have your son die. Thanks for giving us Jeff, for his smile, his laugh, his jokes, and the life he brought to all of us. Amen."

Mrs. Alexander smiled through her tears. She asked what jokes Jeff told, and Bryce got the digital recorder out. We laughed till we cried, then laughed some more.

Mom and Sam came over later, and we all sat up late telling Jeff stories.

I went to the bathroom for some tissues to wipe my eyes and passed Jeff's room. On a whim, I opened the nightstand by his bed and found a notebook with a pen attached to the spiral.

Inside I found a passage about me.

> I wish I could tell somebody how I feel about Ashley. Maybe Bryce would understand. I hope I can get up enough nerve to ask her to the eighth-grade dance next year.

I closed my eyes and the tears came. "I would have said yes," I whispered.

A few pages from the back I found another entry.

> Got a call back from DM today. They said it would be tough keeping all this from Mom and Dad, but that if they had the school's approval, they could go ahead with it. I hope it works out.

CHAPTER 91

☺ *Bryce* ☺

The funeral was small, just the Alexanders and a few friends from church. Because of the media coverage and people from our class, the Alexanders planned a memorial service where everyone could participate.

Jeff looked like he was sleeping, and once I thought how funny it would be if he sat up straight and said, "Just kidding."

The burial at the cemetery was only for the family, but the Alexanders said they wanted Ashley and me and our family there. A slight breeze blew through the trees, and the sun was brilliant. It was a day Jeff would have loved.

I saw Mr. Alexander look at the tree house several times during the service. Our pastor let us say a final good-bye. Then Mr. and Mrs. Alexander spent a few minutes with Jeff's casket. There were lots of tears, but the overall feel of the whole day was hope. We were grieving, but I knew I would see Jeff again.

I looked at Sam and Leigh. They didn't have the same belief in God or the hope I did, and it hurt. I wondered what it would take to get them to believe.

On the way to our car, the Alexanders handed me the videodisc the police had found in the old house. "We haven't figured out how to watch this, and it has your name on it."

"I'll make you a copy and give it to you tomorrow at the memorial service," I said.

When we got home, I stuck the disk into our computer and clicked the Play button. At first I thought it wasn't going to play, but then the disk buzzed and a shot of Jeff's bedroom flashed on-screen. In the corner was the time and date—it was a couple of days before he left for the bike trip.

Jeff plopped on the bed. He had a towel around his neck and was smiling. "Guess if you've found this I'm not around anymore. The way I'm feeling, I'm not sure I'll make it through the bike ride. If I do, it'll be a miracle.

"I knew you'd figure out that I took my own stuff." He held up a key. "Mom and Dad don't know I have this. It's to the trophy room. Do you know why I took the stuff? Well, there's one more surprise for you.

"There're actually two answers to the memorabilia thing. I'm using it for a project you'll find out about. But there's another reason. See, I know it's gonna be hard for my mom and dad after I go. Unlike you, I'm the only one in my family. I know how much you and

Ashley like mysteries, and I told my parents about it. I figured they'd ask you guys to get involved, which means you'll be snooping around. I think it'll help to have you at my house."

Jeff paused and smiled. He was always thinking, but I had no idea how much he had been looking out for his parents.

"Just one more thing. You'll go through the eighth grade and into high school, make a lot of new friends and all that, so it'll probably be easy to just move on. Don't forget me."

I touched the screen. "Not a chance."

CHAPTER 92

❀ Ashley ❀

At the memorial service the next day, people stood and told what Jeff meant to them. It was neat to see so many kids from school who weren't Christians and didn't go to church. Just one more thing Jeff did that amazed me.

Teachers stepped to the microphone and tearfully talked about him. Our youth pastor, Andy, told a couple of really funny stories of things Jeff had said and done.

Mr. Alexander stepped forward and thanked everyone for their support and kindness. He held a piece of paper given to him by the people in the bike ride. When he read the figure, everybody clapped. "The newspaper says even more people are giving in Jeff's memory."

After Jeff's dad sat down, I thought the pastor would conclude the service. Instead, a man in a blue suit stood. He said something to Jeff's dad, then walked to the podium.

Everyone got quiet as the man began. "My name is Tim Minaro, and I'm here on behalf of Dream Makers. We're a group that helps deserving kids realize some dream they've had. Many want to go to Disney World or meet someone famous. But Jeff Alexander was different." He looked at Jeff's mom and dad. "In fact, one of the things he asked us to do was keep this secret from everyone, even his parents. So, if you'd like to see Jeff's dream, meet at the middle school after the service is over."

I looked at Bryce. "DM. Dream Makers."

CHAPTER 93

☻ *Bryce* ☻

I had put everything together except what was under the tarp outside the middle school.

Ashley pointed out a construction guy standing in front of the structure. "That's the Jeppeson guy."

A crowd filled the front of the parking lot as Tim Minaro stood on the back of a truck. Mr. Alexander handed him the box of stuff we had found at the haunted house.

Tim held a megaphone and clicked it on. "Ladies and gentlemen, what you're about to see is the fastest fulfillment of a wish in the history of our organization. Our only regret is that Jeff couldn't be here to see it. One of the things he told us was that there wasn't that much to do in Red Rock."

Everyone laughed.

"He said he wanted to give something to his friends and the kids who would come after him. With the help of Jeppeson Construction, this is the last wish of Jeff Alexander."

The man pulled a string on the side of the tarp revealing a huge climbing wall. The crowd gasped when they saw that the wall was ridged at the top to look like the nearby red rocks. Around the base was a soft rubber pit. The wall was built so that you could climb on either side, and there were colored handholds all the way up.

I moved closer and saw something built into different levels of the climb. Insets in the wall housed footballs, baseballs, all the memorabilia Jeff had collected over the past few months. There were some empty spaces, and I guessed that's what they were going to use the stuff in the box for.

"Is Bryce Timberline here?" Tim said.

I stepped forward and people clapped. The man helped me into the harness you wear when you climb. "Jeff said if he couldn't be here, you should be the first to climb to the top."

I looked back at all my friends, at Ashley and the rest of my family, and got a lump in my throat. Jeff knew I don't really like heights, and though the climbing wall was safe, I felt a sudden panic. I took the first few grips quickly and was about five feet off the ground. The top of the wall looked a million miles away.

At 10 feet, I saw the letter from the president and read the whole thing. I kept moving, past the Elway football and Carmelo basketball. I made the mistake of looking down and nearly quit. It felt like I was on Mount Everest.

I closed my eyes, reached out my hand, and pulled myself up to the next rung.

"You can do it, Bryce!" I heard Dylan shout from below.

"Go, Bryce!" Jeff's mom shouted.

It was all the encouragement I needed.

At the top of the wall, in the middle, was a built-in ledge where you could sit and look at the view. I set my eyes on it and didn't look down again. When I pulled myself to a sitting position and turned around, everybody clapped and cheered. I raised both fists to the sky.

It was then that I noticed a piece of paper taped over the ridge. I pulled it off and opened it.

> Bryce,
>
> You've been a great riding partner and friend. I wish I could be there with you right now, but trust me, I've got a view of my own that's pretty incredible. Looking forward to seeing you soon.
>
> Your friend,
> Jeff

I put the paper down and wiped my eyes. It was almost as if Jeff were speaking to me from the grave, though I knew he'd probably dictated the note by phone while we were on our ride.

I looked at Pikes Peak in the distance and the front range of mountains. The sun lit everything so brightly that it looked like a picture.

I was about to climb down when I realized Jeff's letter had covered something built into the wall. It was a plaque with Jeff's picture. He was smiling that trademark smile of his.

Underneath the plaque was this verse:

A friend is always loyal, and a brother is born to help in time of need.

I looked at the sky through blurry eyes. There weren't any birds or seagulls flying. No angels singing or music playing. Just the sound of a hundred kids saying, "It's my turn!"

EPILOGUE

✱ Ashley ✱

Gunnar was spotted a few days later at a casino west of Denver. Someone recognized him from his photo in the paper, and the police took him into custody, I guess to protect him from the goons. Bryce and I hope he gets help and turns things around.

Hayley and her aunt thanked us for what we did, but we said it wasn't that big of a deal. We love solving mysteries, even if they don't all have happy endings.

The total raised from Jeff's ride was more than $100,000. The newspaper says that figure could go higher.

Every time a kid climbs the wall, they see a little of Jeff's life and read the verse that meant so much to him. After Jeff died, we noticed some people at church who had never been there before.

Every person's life—no matter how long or short—touches others. We were lucky to call Jeff Alexander our friend.

Our lives will never be the same.

About the Authors

Jerry B. Jenkins (jerryjenkins.com) is the writer of the Left Behind series. He owns the Jerry B. Jenkins Christian Writers Guild, an organization dedicated to mentoring aspiring authors. Former vice president for publishing for the Moody Bible Institute of Chicago, he also served many years as editor of *Moody* magazine and is now Moody's writer-at-large.

His writing has appeared in publications as varied as *Reader's Digest, Parade, Guideposts,* in-flight magazines, and dozens of other periodicals. Jenkins's biographies include books with Billy Graham, Hank Aaron, Bill Gaither, Luis Palau, Walter Payton, Orel Hershiser, and Nolan Ryan, among many others. His books appear regularly on the *New York Times, USA Today, Wall Street Journal,* and *Publishers Weekly* best-seller lists.

Jerry is also the writer of the nationally syndicated sports story comic strip *Gil Thorp,* distributed to newspapers across the United States by Tribune Media Services.

Jerry and his wife, Dianna, live in Colorado and have three grown sons and three grandchildren.

Chris Fabry is a writer and broadcaster who lives in Colorado. He has written more than 40 books, including collaboration on the Left Behind: The Kids series.

You may have heard his voice on Focus on the Family, Moody Broadcasting, or Love Worth Finding. He has also written for Adventures in Odyssey and Radio Theatre.

Chris is a graduate of the W. Page Pitt School of Journalism at Marshall University in Huntington, West Virginia. He and his wife, Andrea, have been married 22 years and have nine children, two birds, two dogs, and one cat.

RED ROCK MYSTERIES

BRYCE AND ASHLEY TIMBERLINE are normal 13-year-old twins, except for one thing—they discover action-packed mystery wherever they go. Wanting to get to the bottom of any mystery, these twins find themselves on a nonstop search for truth.

CP0140